Copyright © 2015 (

All rights re:

ISBN: 9798358701779

Cover design by: Jaide Bradley
Edited by: Caitlin Bradley
Library of Congress Control Number: 2018675309
Printed in the United States of America

*This book is dedicated to my mother and father,
Rosemary and Charles Bradley. The entire family circle,
the angels – Kieran Hawkins, Kieran CB Hawkins, Conor
Bradley, Sona- Therese Bradley and Kevin Bradley.
Also, the good people of Ardoyne, The Bone and Ligoniel
who worked in the mills.
I hope you enjoy this story about our ancestors as much
as I did.
Yours Sincerely,
Conor Bradley*

CONTENTS

NEXT STOP HEAVEN

by Cahal Bradley

✽ ✽ ✽

FOREWORD

My name is Conor Bradley, grandson of author Cahal Bradley. I have previously published Next Stop Heaven in 2015 and shared the story with the people of Ardoyne and its surrounding communities. I sold 1000 copies of this much-loved tale and was content with knowing my Grandfathers manuscript had been enjoyed by the people of his origin. For the past few years, I have been searching for family in New York.

One week following my registration on Ancestry I found a great nephew of Cahal Bradley, the Grandson of Hugh Bradley, Mike McDermott. During our conversations I told him of Next Stop Heaven. It was then that he informed me of an unpublished manuscript written by Hugh Bradley, a tale also set in the same era and place, Old Belfast.

On receiving Hugh's manuscript, I told Mike he should pursue publication of the book. We have now joined together to publish the manuscripts of the two brothers, which both lay undiscovered for many decades, hoping to share their literature with all of Ireland and beyond.

- Conor Bradley

PREFACE

For over fifty years the Bradley family from Ardoyne had a secret and treasured heirloom which is finally seeing the light of day.

It is a treasure trove but not of the monetary kind. Its value is to be found in the joy it brings to the extended Bradley family, in its words, its ideas, in the link it provides to a past long gone, but still has relevance to the extended family of the author and indeed, to many people who appreciate history and the insight it gives us to the time and the lives of those who came before us.

Conor Bradley is the third generation in possession of the family legacy. His father Charles was the second and his father Cahal was the first. Conor has passionately pursued the unveiling of the heirloom over the last five years in memory of his father and in tribute to his grandfather Cahal Bradley who is the author of the treasured novel.

Cahal Bradley, who today is largely unknown outside of his family and his native Ardoyne, but he was not an insignificant public figure, in the political, historical, cultural, literary and business life of Belfast between 1900 and his death in 1957.

This legacy, which has been documented in newspapers and books, can now be added to, with a hitherto unpublished manuscript of a true love story, filled with the hard-hitting themes of tough labour and the importance of a caring souled community. The novel is based on the life of Cahal Bradley's father, Charles, who is Conor Bradley's great grandfather.

The manuscript which is now published as a book is called, 'Next Stop Heaven'. Cahal Bradley wrote the story, which is set in a small, tight knit village, which is situated in Ardoyne, beneath the Black Mountain, 300 meters distance from the Holy Cross Chapel.

Next Stop Heaven' profiles the lives of a group of families who live in Ravages Row, Richell's Row and Crosses Row. They are mill workers and the author regularly describes them as 'slaves' to the mill owners. This represents the degrading discrimination which was inflicted against the working people of the area, in the late 19th century.

The book is set in a time when children as young as 11 worked in the mills; when lives were shortened by ill-health from their working conditions and when the only relief, from life's drudgery was the beloved Chapel, the mountain and for some, alcohol. In fact, it added to the miserable plight of families because husbands drank much-needed money.

Cahal Bradley relies a lot on contrast to emphasis his social commentary. The working conditions within the Mills involved heinous pay, health thieving long hours and poisonous air. Cahal uses this horrendous imagery in contrast to the enormous, mighty mountain, which contained beautiful, memory holding land, imprinted with the footsteps of lovers and nourished with the tears of the broken hearted. This contrast allows us to notice the two sides of life which the villagers experienced. The mountain is also referred to the 'massive motionless dark green colored whale' by the author and narrator Cahal Bradley himself.

Nature and the home of one of the book's main characters, Johnny Connor, which is a picturesque cottage set on the mountain side, is a constant backdrop where all good happens and where mill workers go to relax, have their batteries recharged and where love flourishes.

Example Of Mill Worker - Circa 1870

The book's love story based on the characters Sheila and Ned unfolds against the threat posed to it by immigration. We get a sense of people struggling, politically and economically, through the debates that take place between the mill workers, the clergy and the well-off over the merits of protesting and organising for social change or acceptance of one's lot in this life.

The author's patriotic sentiments are also reflected as is his opposition to sectarianism which is clear in the scene were riots occur between Catholics and Protestants. The book is very well written and the description of many of the scenes are detailed and vivid and reflect the mind of a man who is a socialist and a patriot.

The mind of a man who spent many years as a political activist in the IRA and Sinn Féin and other nationalist organisations. Cahal Bradley was born in Ardoyne on 7th February 1886. He was christened Charles after his father. By the age of 16 he spoke Irish fluently and used the Irish version of his name Cahal O'Brallaghan. He was one of five children, including his siblings, Hugh, Margaret, Peter and Annie.

Their parents, Charles Bradley a Fenian leader, was born in Buncrana on the Inishowen Peninsula, Margaret McGreevy, was born Kilkeel, in county Down.

The Bradley family are registered as living in Brookfield Street in Ardoyne in 1901. The census register shows that other Bradleys', Peter, William and James also lived in Ardoyne at this time.

They were all related and came from Donegal to Belfast in the late 19th century.

The first known record of the Bradley family's knowledge of Cahal's involvement in Irish affairs was when Cahal and his father, alongside a few other men formed the Charles Kickham GAA club in Ardoyne, in August 1907. Its inaugural meeting was held in Cahal's home at 16 Leopold Street. A record of the minute of the meeting shows that Cahal, at the age of 21, was its secretary and his father Charles was its first chairperson.

Kickhams Team - Cahal Top Row Left Wearing Hat

Cahal and his two brothers, Hugh and Peter were actively involved in the Irish Republican Brotherhood and IRA and nationalist organisations like Sinn Féin, the National Council and after partition the Anti-Partitionist League.

Cahal moved to Derry in 1919 where he lived for several years and married Mary Louisa McKnight. They had four children, all boys. While there he was a leading member of Sinn Féin and was the first Nationalist Deputy Lord Mayor in Derry City council set up after partition.

At the Derry city's first council meeting after the 1920 local government election Cahal proudly seconded a motion to remove the Union Jack which was flying over the council offices. In an act of reconciliation towards the unionists and Protestants of Derry the nationalist council also agreed not to fly any flags including the Irish tricolour. He also proposed a motion rejecting the jurisdiction of the unionist parliament while pledging loyalty to Dáil Eireann.

Derry Corp Council - Cahal Front Row Third From Left

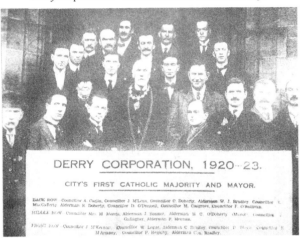

Cahal and his family returned to Ardoyne in 1926. The reason for their return, was to run the family business in Herbert Street, where they lived. The family run business was a grocery store which was also exporting carrageen moss to America; this was a special type of seaweed found in coastline areas of the North Atlantic, one of which was along the Derry seafronts.

The seaweed was an important ingredient in some foodstuffs and also useful in medicinal products.

When the last of the Bradleys moved out of Herbert street, they donated the row of houses that they built to the community; this is where the people of Ardoyne were enabled to open the first Ardoyne Community Centre.

The partition of Ireland and the subsequent Civil War broke up the national independence movement and led to the nationalist people of the north being abandoned to their fate at the hands of the sectarian unionist state and its political and armed forces.

During this period Cahal met Eamon de Valera and Michael Collins seeking their support for the beleaguered nationalist people of Derry and Ardoyne.

A letter written by his brother Hugh in 1950 while living in New York, to the Irish government seeking a service medal, which was available to ex-members of the Irish Volunteers or Irish Citizen Army, provides a very interesting insight to the circumstances in which the war for freedom was waged and the level that Hugh operated at during the period from 1915 - 1921.

The letter written in Hugh's own hand, states that while he was interned in Ballykinlar for a year in 1921 he was beaten by British soldiers and the injuries led to a nervous breakdown. He was unable to work for many years after his release from prison.

To support his application for his service medal he referred to his role as an IRA volunteer organising the IRA in north Belfast, Tyrone, Down and Armagh. During the years between 1917-21 he referred in his letter, to being in the company of Eamon de Valera, Countess Markievicz, Bulmer Hobson, Eoin McNeill, Boland, Cahoon and Fitzgerald - many of these republicans were leading figures in the War of Independence, the Civil War and post-partition Irish politics.

Cahal Bradley was elected as a member of the Anti-Partition League to the Senate at Stormont and between 1951 and 1957 the Senate's records show him participating in many debates on the economic and political impact of partition on the people of Ireland.

In his first recorded debate in 1951 he argued for more trade between the north and south, the future of the Great Northern Railway; the harassment of passengers on this line by British custom officials; the cost to the local economy of exporting cattle on the hoof to Britain; the burden on people of high taxes on cigarettes and alcohol compared to the cost of both in the south; the protection of small businesses and the partisan use of the RUC as a force to maintain partition.

Prior to Next Stop Heaven, he had also published two books. The first book he published was named 'Parishes of Ireland'. The second book which he had written, In 1931, was a book called, 'Songs of a Commercial Traveler'. The poems, some 80 in total reflect the ups and downs of life on the road as a travelling salesman, which Cahal was in his early years. In addition to his writing career, he was an accomplished historian; Cahal was a man who was concerned with the research of past events. In addition to this, he also wrote a column for the Irish News.

The soul of Cahal Bradley is conveyed through the life and imprint that he has left behind in each poem and novel he has created. His long life of determination, leadership, deep interest in his country and creative imagination is what influenced his career as an author. Although to some, he would have been known as a mighty, powerful man, his emotions and life experiences are almost shared to those whom have read and understood his work.

My favourite poem of many favourites might capture the spirit of Cahal O'Brallaghan and the challenging yet heroic times he lived through and by his actions in the IRA and Sinn Féin and his dedication to serving his community he helped shape the Ireland of his day.

Those of us trying to shape the Ireland of today would do well to read about Cahal and reflect on the sentiment in his poem, 'The Struggle is the thing to make a Chap'.

- Preface by Jim Gibney

THE STRUGGLE IS THE THING TO MAKE A CHAP

THERE'S joy in ev'ry hour if we can find it,
There's joy in ev'ry moment of the day;
The sorrow-cloud has got a joy behind it,
A happy hear can make December – May.

The one who looks for blooms is sure to find them,
The one who fingers nettles will be stung;
A wise man puts unpleasant things behind him,
And muddles on believing he is young.

There's luck in life for him that keeps on trying –
The razor is the sharper for the strap –
And though you're left with nought to will on dying
The struggle is the thing to make a chap.

- Cahal Bradley - 1931

TRANSLATIONS

Some of the character's names and places have been changed by the author.

"Bad scran to ye" -

A curse of ill luck.

"Ploucher" -

Trouble.

"Deal table" -

Soft wood or pine.

"No Goat's Toe" -

Not stupid.

"Feth" -

Replacement of swear word.

"(A) cad" -

Someone who knows right from wrong but struggles to live by the differences.

"Brochan" -

Sweet words from a rotten mouth (person).

"Yoked" -

Attached.

"Tender" -

A frame maker.

"Your till a cinder" -

Signing of a letter.

"A drudge" -

A persona made to do hard, menial or dull work.

"Gridiron" -

Frame of metal bars used for grilling fish or meat (over open fire).

"Vexed" -

Mad, angry or displeased.

"Cur" -

A contemptible man.

"Ague" -

Illness involving fever or shivering.

"Din" -

Loud and unpleasant noise.

"Tholings" -

Suffering.

"Pluck" -

Spirited and determined courage.

"Doffers" -

Mill worker who clears spindles of old fibre.

"Demurred" -

Raise objections or show reluctance.

"Lithe" -

Thin, supple and graceful (especially of a person's body).

"Bough" -

Main branch of a tree.

"Loanin" -

A lane.

"Lauded" -

Praise a person of their achievements.

"Coltsfoot" -

Any plants (with large petals) resembling a Colt's foot.

"Fiendish noises" -

Extremely cruel or unpleasant noises.

"Countenance" -

Face.

CHAPTER ONE

Johnny Connor's

L ike a massive motionless dark green coloured whale towering in the sky to the height of 1,400 feet the Black Mountain or Dark Hill as it is called, rests above the town of Belfast. From above where one might imagine the green whales head to start a narrow white lane, that takes its name of the White Road from a surface of white stones and blocks of white limestone in the neighbourhood, runs almost straight down towards the City of Linen in the broad valley below. At the top of the road Johnny Connor resided. Like the mountain Johnny was dark, tall and broad. From mountainy land his fathers before him had dragged a living and although he had been given a good schooling Johnny asked for no better. A small yellow thatched snow-white cottage that seemed to cling in terror, to the steep side of the dark mountain, a few acres almost entirely of heather and rock covered land, a horse and cart, five cows, a number of fowl, and an ailing wife and a quiet girl of fifteen years, were all of Johnny's earthly possessions, and as he would have said himself they were "enough with a blessing."

Between Johnny's cabin and the top of the hill there was no other house and being so close to the summit the people of the town who braved the climb after their work in the stuffy mills used to jokingly call the hillman's home "Next Stop Heaven" a name given to it by Peter Brady the hackler. The remainder of the broad expanse of the massive motionless dark green whale was just rugged mountain with the tail of the monster appearing to twine into the Clift, at the Hill of Wolves above Ligoniel. From the door of his humble cottage that looked down on the River Lagan, Johnny had a perfect view of the town of Belfast as it spread itself on either side of the River Lagan. Owing to the steepness of the slope, no tree or bush stretched high enough to obstruct the vision.

In the early summer of the year 1879, Belfast, like many other industrial towns, was suffering from the growing pains and from his elevated position Johnny Connor was able to watch its stretching antics and even hear of its increasing mill horns and hum of its machinery's agonising roar. It had gone crazy on linen. When he opened the cabin door each morning his first glance was to see if any changes had taken places in the town's formation from the previous day and in that early look there was always an expression of pity or anger rather than admiration. The laying-out of another new street, the marking of foundations for another mill, the erection of another huge chimney or the arrival of another strange boat in the docks; these were continual surprises for the big mountainy man, whose "God help them" could have almost been heard in the stuffy mills but for the noise of the machinery.

"Chuckie, chuckie, chuckie," echoed over the dark hill on this afternoon as rattling a large tin against the gable of the house, Johnny Connor directed these magic words towards the heathery slopes.

"Chuckie, chuckie, chuckie," he repeated until the heather seemed to take legs and hens, ducks and geese came charging down, from all angles towards the cabin.

"There ye are," shouted the mountainy man still banging his tin against the wall and addressing a handsome young clergyman who leaned on the half-door of the cabin.

"There ye are, Father, it's what I tell ye, hens are just like human beings and it's the rattle of the tin that draws them, they're just like the poor working creatures who come to the town below."

The rough yard echoed to the strong voice. As he moved and spoke the hillman closely watched by this reverend friend who stood comparing in his own mind the strong arms and sturdy frame of the speaker to his own neglected body. An ardent student of Irish history he fancied the mountainy man was like as an ancient warrior chieftain alive again in modern life.

"We're a home loving people and none of us want to leave our homes in this country", continued Johnny.

The hens were the first to arrive in the yard beside the house. Flinging handfuls of yellow meal amongst them Johnny continued.

"Them fowl would far sooner stay on the hill above, but the rattle of the tin tells them there's more food for them down here. It's just like that, Father. There's hungry human beings all over the country and the rattle of the machinery ye be hearing in the town is just the tin to them."

As the man of the mountain talked the fowl surged around his feet.

"Then you don't call it progress, Johnny?" asked the priest, his eyes travelling over the smoking town below.

"Progress be damned," sharply answered his friend, pitching a handful of food among the birds. "I call it promise not progress. It's just another question of a feeding place. People go where there's a promise of more food, but that doesn't mean they'll get it. Over the country where starvation's hounding them from their wee bits of farms the poor people are glad to hear of any sort of noise or listen to any kind of promise."

Continuing to feed his interested flock, the hillman scowled down at the mills, while the young priest looked on in amusement.

"Chuckie, chuckie, chuckie," louder roared Johnny, this time directing his call far over the heather. Bang, bang, bang went the tin.

"They're some slow of coming, father. We call them the slow-pack." Johnny added almost to himself, "They wonder far."

"Maybe they're hard of hearing," said the clergyman dryly. The man of the mountain smiled but continued roaring until all the birds had arrived.

"You've some fine birds there Johnny," remarked his reverence moving towards the assembled flock.

"Feth, they wouldn't be fine for long if they didn't get their grub," said the feeder stopping at his work to examine the far-off heather searchingly.

Apparently satisfied that no stragglers had been left

behind he looked again towards the town, as he scattered more meal.

"And that's what I do be thinking father about those poor people who are coming to live in that dingy town below. The machinery there may hum out plenty of promises of food, but God help them it's more than food they'll be getting I'll warrant ye. They'll be made to pay dearly for the wee bits of crumbs with their health and character, for the call of 'come and feed' nowadays is just a call of 'come and slave'."

"But, Johnny," queried the clergyman with a slight smile on his lips "you know man must work."

"Yes, yes, that's all very well," his friend impatiently retorted, "but surely ye don't call the unrewarded slavery that goes on in those mills by the holy name of work. Surely a man of your education and training should know better than all that."

The priest laughed loudly. He had already become accustomed to the mountainy man's attacks. Flinging the meal faster to the fowl Johnny heard his laugh and grunted.

"Damn all else I say it is but taking a mean advantage of the poor helpless people in order to build up stinking mills and fill lousy purses."

Suddenly the hillman stopped his work and dramatically pointing towards the big mills in the distance, shouted rather than spoke.

"God never decreed that mankind should be locked up in yon hellish prisons or packed in such choked measly houses. Poor things they are hardly allowed to look into a garden and almost every field is barred to them. The only place they can put their tired feet on green grass is on this mountain-top and if ye only saw the joy a tiny bit of heather or wildflower can give them when they do come up here ye would never forget it. God knows it's a poor way for decent people to have to live in this supposed enlightened age."

Almost exhausted by his outburst the big man approached the priest. Wetting his lips with his tongue he strove to speak with some control, "They're all of good blood, father, well-bred of a race of good fathers and mothers, and come from the evicted farms in the neighbouring counties, it's a great pity of them," then shaking his head rather sadly at the lines of the streets and mills below he added tearfully, "God help them father, God help them and everybody like them who have to wait on wheels and horns for a living."

The priest was about to say something but Johnny's sudden roar of, "Jinny, Jinny, Jinny," stopped his words. What on earth, he thought was Jinny. Then watching his strange friend he noticed another bucket had been secured and that the hillman was striding though the fowl towards a small green gate opening into the heather from the yard. Flinging the gate wide open Johnny banged his bucket against the gatepost, at the same time roaring, "Jinny, Jinny," towards the hill.

The priest had not long to wait in his wondering. In a few seconds the maned head of a brown mare appeared high up at the summit. The animal came charging down through the heather and whins. Arriving in the yard it gleefully pranced round its owner and then pushed its nose deep into the bucket, while Johnny talked to it and patted its neck and shoulders.

"You've got her well trained anyhow Johnny," remarked the priest admiringly, at the same time moving away from the mare.

"It's the rattle of the tin all over again," answered Johnny, patting Jinny and adding with a smile.

"She always comes when she hears it, she loves me for the food I give her."

"No, Johnny, I wouldn't say that. You have given that mare more than food by the looks of her - you have given her kindness."

The mountainy man was pleased and showed his pleasure by patting the brown mare more affectionately. Then turning to the priest, he feelingly replied, "Poor Jinny she's just another good sort of slave and nothing more."

"Does she not enjoy her servitude in such good company?" questioned the priest.

Johnny looked at the mare as he drawled, "She tries to God help her - she's plucky - like poor Peter Brady, the hackler down in the town - but she has her hard days to go through all the same." Hanging the bucket on the gatepost he left the animal to its food and walked towards the house saying - "I was near forgetting, father, I have kept a dozen fresh eggs and a print of butter for ye to take back with ye."

The priest trotted after his friend and waited at the door of the cabin until he returned from the kitchen with a neat little basket in his hand.

"Here ye are, father," reaching the basket, "and I hope you'll enjoy them."

With a deluge of thanks Father Mick took the eggs and butter and bidding his friend, "Good day and God's blessing," set out on his journey back to the town.

At the spring mountain well with its cool sparkling water he was tempted to drink and leaving his treasured basket on the ground so far forgot his dignity as to lie down on his belly in order that his nose and lips might reach the water. In spite of this inconvenience, he drank well and long and rising wiped his face with his dark red coloured handkerchief.

A young man of thirty years, Father Mick had come to the Belfast monastery of the Passionist Fathers at Ardoyne some months previously. Only a short time a priest, the earnest desire to become a good one burned strongly in his veins, and he tried hard to love everybody. He had not been stationed there more than a week when he discovered that Johnny Connor was the one member of his congregation who could supply fresh eggs and butter straight from the farm, so, soon after his arrival the young priest and the mountainy man had become fast friends, and the steep white road to the dark hill had become Father Mick's favourite walk.

Coming, as he did, from county Tyrone and being the son of a struggling small farmer he and Johnny Connor, having much in common, often met to talk about the farming country and the growing town with its fast-increasing number of workers that as Mick McLaverty would say was "stealing the green fields."

Carrying his basket with care lest the jolting on the rough road might break the eggs, he walked cautiously down the steep white path while between watching the eggs and having an occasional hurried glance at the scenery he found himself at times, recalling some of the things his mountainy friend had said.

Stretching in the distance before him he could see the River Lagan and the blue hills of Down where Patrick had spent so many years - and then it flashed on him that even Patrick the Saint of the Irish had been a slave. Away to his left towered the grim commanding Hill of the Caves, known as Cavehill and when permitted by the rough road to lift his mind from the eggs, the young priest's eyes darted towards the broad dark mound with its Phrygian cap. There, he knew in the high fort the great McArt O'Neill had held court in bygone years. As he tried to picture the grandeur of such display, he fancied he saw crowds of hungry faces peep out from the trees that lines the slopes. The glory of the great occasion was disturbed by the ghosts of slaves and beggars.

A noise in the basket, caused by his ankle bending on a stone, chased the picture from his mind fearing that some of his eggs had been broken he stopped. Satisfied however, that only a small dinge on one egg had been the cause of the noise the priest pursued his journey. Half-way down the steep road his eyes scanned the hill to the right, and the memory of a fighting O'Neill entertaining in his Castle of The Eagle's Nest, came only to be disturbed by the thoughts of starving hundreds thronging near the gates for "leavings".

"Slaves, slaves, slaves and Abraham Lincolns dead" Johnny Connor would have said and haunted by thoughts of slaves and Johnny's sayings he heard the hum of the machinery in the mills and remembered the men and women and boys and girls locked up with the noise and dust on such a beautiful day. From far behind the repeating call of a bird on the hill seemed to say, "they're building on sand, they're building on sand."

On his walk down the steep white road he had travelled through the years to meet the fact that the past was gone and here he was in the machinery present. His sturdy friend was on the dark hill above and he himself had reached the door of the Old House, the priest's house. The hill above, he thought, seemed in the past.

Before entering it, he took another look into his little basket. "Fresh butter and eggs" he murmured to himself with thankfulness, "what a blessing, what a blessing!"

CHAPTER TWO

The Old House

A kindly soul was how the workers, living at the foot of the big dark hill, described Father Mick. Somehow, they knew his heart did not warm to the exploiting and that they had his sympathy and prayers; and it was whispered around that his father was a poor struggling farmer who had laboured long and hard on his land to keep his son off it. In this the parent had succeeded, his greatest reward being the belief that his boy would thus escape the cruelties of the system in a monastery, and by so escaping might save his soul and incidentally help the souls of his family and their friends. The boy became a priest, and the father went on slaving and damning on his unprofitable bit of bog land.

Some sons might have forgotten their fathers' struggle, but the young priest was not one of these. To him the land always spoke of his parents and loving his father and mother he loved the land. It was because of this that he loved the heather around Johnny Connor's white cottage on the dark hill and disliked the narrow dirty streets around the smelling mills.

At the Old House or Monastery in Ardoyne he was now living. It was a strange place. Formerly, it had been a public-house where the clink of glasses and the coarse language of drunken men resounded. Now it was the home of missioners and a house of prayer.

The name of "The Black Doctor's" by which it had formerly been known had, with the arrival of the priests, given place to "The Old House."

The Publican who had been called Black Doctor because of claims he made to working miracles by his liquor was supplanted by a number of religious men proclaiming to work them by prayer and faith.

To this old building which was, what in those days, would have been described as a gentleman's residence, the priests had removed from a modest little one-storey thatched cottage. When doing so one of the mill workers engaged in carrying their furniture was heard to remark "I hope this won't change them into snobs, in the wee cottage they were like ourselves."

Situated about half-way between the centre of the town and Johnny Connor's cottage on the hill the Old House was just above the mills and convenient to the rows of workers houses. When the first priests, under the vow of poverty, came to live in the small one-storey cottage the members of the congregation, almost all of whom were mill-workers, hated to see them in such a humble residence. The poor people did not want their clergy to be as restricted as themselves and so endeavoured to push them up amongst the gentry for safety. The Old House was therefore the result of the first push, so, if in subsequent years many of the old workers expressed surprise that some of the clergy on their part had not volunteered alike assistance in workers' battles, it is not to be wondered at.

Out of all proportion to their lot in life the poor folk lavished kindness upon them and rallying to their support took pride in each improvement of their circumstances. They simply went mad in their efforts to drag the missioners out of their apparent poverty thus forgetting their own, and anyone who visits Belfast today can see how successful they have been.

Ardoyne, which was then a tree covered hill, is now one of the beauty spots of Ireland and the twin-spired church and huge monastery that adorn its hill are among the most substantial of edifices. At least the appearances of priestly poverty have disappeared, but the workers still have little security.

After the priests had secured the Old House and its grounds the workers, although weary from their long labour in the mills, rushed from their homes each evening to feel trees in order to make room for the erection of a church. Out of their lean purses money flowed to be added to by the collections organised far and near by the girls from the spinning and weaving rooms. Soon a church arose, schools were built, gardens made, and many conveniences provided for the clergymen.

But to resume our story. We left Father Mick standing at the door of the Old House inspecting the small basket of eggs he had carried down so carefully from the cottage on the top of the dark hill. Delighted with his present and satisfied he had carried it safely to his destination the young priest opened the front door of the building and passed into the large dark hall.

In the shadow he saw the shawled figure of a thin woman. The shawl, which was tightly drawn over her head, was black and torn. Immediately she recognised the priest the woman curtsied and in a quiet apologetic voice said.

"I hope ye'll forgive me for troubling ye, Father."

"It's quite alright, my child," replied the priest assuringly.

Conscious of the smell of the mills that permeated the hall his reverence sniffed. Then he noticed the tow that struck on various parts of the woman's torn shawl.

"Ye know me, Father," the woman meekly continued, loosening the shawl and drawing it back slightly from her pale face.

"I'm Josephine McCann of Ravages Row, -Jimmy McCann's wife, " then fearing the priest did not recognise her, the poor woman reminded him further, "I buried my husband last week and ye were at the funeral."

"Oh yes, oh, yes, I remember," the priest said now recognising the woman. Placing his hand upon her shoulder he asked kindly, "And how are you and your children keeping?"

Mrs. McCann rubbed her eyes with her shawl, "The childer are grand, thank God, Father."

Father Mick noticed she did not speak of herself and looking at the pale pained face and thin figure he found himself thinking of the large poor family with this little woman as its sole provider.

"And how about yourself?" he asked.

The woman brightened. Straightening herself up as if to convey a reserve of strength she answered with, what he thought, a smile on her lips.

"Oh, I'm alright, I'm working every day. I just got out for an hour to come up and see ye."

Father Mick tried to think of what her work might be. He wondered what kind of labour this frail woman could do. He knew she was a spinner and knew she worked from 6.30 in the morning until 6 in the evening, but he had not the remotest idea what her occupation entailed. Clergymen did not visit spinning rooms so he could only pity her for the confinement that her job demanded. He would have liked to have asked what she had to do but as priests were supposed to be learned he did not care to show he knew nothing about it. Instead, he asked, "What can I do for you Mrs. McCann?"

The woman's hands began searching under her shawl and from somewhere near her poorly clad breast she drew out a handful of silver. The priest stood watching as she fumbled, and the smell of the mill grew stronger in the dark hall. Carefully adjusting her shawl Mrs. McCann held the money towards him.

"Here's fifteen shillings, Father, and I want ye to say masses for my poor Jimmy's soul."

"But, my child," remonstrated the priest, "this is far too much." Then thinking of the children he added, "You will need it all and more for your little ones."

The thin hand containing the silver trembled but was extended further from the shawl while a voice that bespoke pain pleaded.

"We all want to help Jimmy. He was good to us and it was

a poor time he had with the bad health on this earth."

Deciding that five shillings would be enough to take, his reverence, reached for the money saying, "I will only take five shillings from you," but the then nervous hand clutched the coins tightly and the woman sobbed.

"No, no, Father, ye must take it all. All we wanted to do in life was to make Jimmy happy and all that Jimmy wanted to do was to make me and the childer happy, the roughing killed him. His lungs never could stand it. "Ye must take it all Father," she pleaded and added beseechingly, "Ye must help him all ye can with yer prayers, God knows it's only too little that we can do for him now."

Father Mick still disliked to take so much from the poor woman for whom he felt deeply.

"Tell me Mrs. McCann" he asked, "Have you any more money besides these fifteen shillings?" But before he had the question completed the woman answered, "No, no, none, but that doesn't matter Father, that doesn't matter. I'll have a pay coming, I'll have a pay coming."

Then drawing nearer to the priest, she looked up at him and again extending the money as if making a final appeal pleaded, "Father, this money isn't mine. It's Jimmy's, It's Jimmy's. It's what was left of his insurance after burying him. We have no right to it. We have no right to it. We couldn't do much for him here, Father," then bursting into tears she cried, "Oh Father he had a poor life of it on earth, for God's sake help him, help him all ya can where he is, help him all ya can where he is."

Father Mick felt a lump gather in his throat as the warm money was pressed into his reluctant hand. When he spoke again his voice was choked. "Alright, my child, God reward him and you, I will say the masses," he said as the woman bowed down gratefully muttering. "Thank ye, Father." Kissing his hand, she tightened her old shawl around her and swept past him out of the door. The silence of her movements made the priest look after the retreating woman as she crossed the school yard and passed the church on her way to the mill. As his eyes followed the dark-shawled figure the absence of noise from its footsteps made him glance towards her feet to discover they were bare. Dazed, he stood thus for a few moments to be suddenly aroused by the sound of a loud voice at his back.

"Well Mick what is it?" it asked, the young priest turned around to meet his superior who was about to go out of the house.

Holding the still warm money on his hand so that his superior might see it, Father Mick looking towards the disappearing figure explained with emotion.

"That poor woman, that woman whom you see going down the steps yonder, that woman with the dark shawl and bare feet, gave me all this money to say masses for her late husband."

His superior did not appear to be impressed. Lifting the money from the extended palm he gave a cough and after complaining about the objectionable smell in the hall said, "You're young on the mission, my son you'll soon get used to such things and you'll find them most amongst the poorest people." and sailed past him without any further comment.

The young priest looked after the portly figure of his superior, the coolness of whose remark had hurt. He was perplexed. Then remembering his basket, he again looked at the eggs. The whiteness of the shells reminded him of the poor woman's pale face. A pain gathered at his heart. Taking the basket, he went across to the school. As he crossed the yard a voice seemed to say, "Pale face, white eggs, pale face, white eggs." Father Mick loved a fresh egg but securing the service of a little altar boy he handed him the basket with these instructions, "Take this down to Mrs. McCann of Ravage's Row and tell her that Father Michael sent it for herself and her children."

CHAPTER THREE

Ravage's Row

T he little boy whom Father Mick sent with the eggs and butter to Mrs. McCann's home had not far to go. About two hundred yards further down the broad road stood a group of high mills. Beneath them three rows of very small, lime-washed kitchen houses harboured the workers. They were called Ravage's Row, Richhell's Row, and Crosses Row, and in appearance were much alike, the houses in each being as small as it was possible to build them. In one of these tiny homes, in Ravage's Row, the rougher Jimmy McCann had lived and died.

Some thirty years earlier Jimmy had arrived in the town of Belfast with the soft pleasant words of County Armagh upon his boyish tongue, but after a few years of long hours in the noisy mills the machinery chased their softness and left him with the hard accent of the industrial town. In the bug-room soft musical voices did not carry above the noise of the machinery, so the hard sounding notes were adopted by the workers. Even the beauties of speech were surrendered to the machine.

In County Armagh, Jimmy's father had been a farm labourer with a large family of small children. His earnings were very small. As they all had to starve, Jimmy at the age of eleven years left his father's home for Belfast in order to relieve the situation, or as Johnny Connor of the big dark hill used to say; "he heard the rattle of Belfast's machinery with its promise of more food and ran like hell to it."

On the land in Armagh nothing seemed to flourish so well as poverty. Everybody starved so that few might have plenty.

Nobody seemed to understand why. Somebody said it was God's Holy Will so nobody wanted to disturb the order of things for fear of "flying in the face of providence."

Jimmy, like thousands of others, had heard of the "Goings-on" in Belfast and, with a view to easing the burden on his poor father, he decided to try and relieve himself. With each scanty meal the thought that every bite was depriving the younger members of the family of nourishment had become a daily torture. He also saw his growing appetite was only increasing the strangulation of his already heart-broken father. All this consideration the poor parents must have detected in their son for on his departure to Belfast no mother or father could have wept more bitterly.

Although not a strong lad Jimmy walked the whole way to the town where, soon after his arrival, he got started in the bug-room of one of the mills. In those days that was the name given to the machine room of a Linen Mill, possibly because of the dirt, for it is told a foreman often had to get the boy he was sacking washed in order to know who was being dismissed. Little boys of eleven years wrought in this department and Jimmy was considered lucky to get started.

Eventually he reached the roughing shop and in time became a fully qualified rougher. Then he met Josephine, who like himself had also come from the country with soft words on her tongue and was now a spinner. They courted, were married, and had a family of three girls and two boys. These, when the rougher died, were left at the tender ages of 2, 4, 7, 9 and 17 years. To bring them up both parents had worked their jobs and it was a great consolation to them when Sheila, the eldest girl (now seventeen years), was able to mind the home and look after the smaller children in the parents' absence. Jimmy's burden was just beginning to show promise of being lightened when he died and left the woman he loved with the load.

As the little boy with the butter and eggs from Father Mick entered Ravage's Row a number of children were skipping in front of the McCann's house while near the window four or five little girls were playing baby-dishes with pieces of broken glass and delph obtained by a careful exploration of the dung pits. All of the children were on their bare feet and warmly though poorly dressed.

In trying to enter the McCann's doorway the little boy had to step over the assembled playthings. This annoyed the children, one of whom wickedly yelled.

"Where are ye going big feet?"

While another added swearingly, "God, he thinks he's somebody because he's working for the priests at the big house."

The boy was embarrassed and when no answer came to

his knock stuttered to his attackers, "Does, does any of ye know if Mrs. McCann's in?"

One of the children immediately jumped up from the play and rushing into the hall replied defiantly, "No, she's not, she's at her work"

Then putting her little hands on her hinches she asked with assumed dignity, "What do ye want with her anyhow?"

"B-b-but," stammered the boy, "she was at the priest's house a while ago."

The child puckered her brows then with mischievous smile replied: "Well if she was, she must have asked out from her work?"

While the conversation was going on another little girl with childish curiosity had sneaked behind the boy and uncovered the eggs in his basket. Extracting a large one she ran away with it and dancing tantalizingly on the street began screaming, "Oh, look at the big egg, oh look at the big egg!"

The lad blushed and was preparing to run after the mischievous one when the kitchen door opened and a soft, sweet, young voice asked, "Are ye looking for my ma?"

Recognising Sheila, the eldest daughter of the McCann family, the boy checked himself and shyly reached the basket saying, "Yes Sheila, Father Mick sent this down to yer mother for herself and the childher."

Sheila McCann took the basket and, thanking the lad

began calling to the mischievous little one to bring back the egg, as the messenger with evident relief, hurried out of the street.

The girl to whom the eggs and butter were delivered was the prettiest thing in Ravage's Row, in fact she was the prettiest thing in all the mill district. Old men loved to look at her and the young men, too shy to look, hoped she'd look at them. Sheila McCann was just seventeen but there was something about her that made her age not matter and made both old and young men forget theirs. Even the millowner's son when he passed her, forgot his station and that she lived in such a place as Ravage's Row. Her clothes may not have been attractive, but Sheila shone, over and beyond what she wore! In her movements there was warmth and poetry and graces. Because of her lovely, dimpled cheeks her school companions nick-named her "Dimples" but by the elder people she was called Sheila.

As her lithe young figure passed up and down the street her bright kindly Irish eyes played hide-and-seek beneath dancing dark curls and blinds were pulled aside for admiring peeps to reach her. But in Sheila there was something more than looks. The neighbours loved her and a very common reference to her was "she's an angel" while others said "The nicest thing about her is that she doesn't know she's so lovely."

Everybody, particularly on a Sunday, when she wore her good frock and hat, had eyes for her, but there was only one young man in the district the sight of whom could make the girl's heart creep up into her eyes. Sheila worshipped him but like the shy girl she was, at a distance. Of him, she often thought and for him she would proudly preserve and protect all she had to give. From her poverty she could not gather money, but she would keep her lips, her arms, her mind, her love for him and for him alone, and she often secretly prayed that he might someday consider that wealth enough. To no one else but him would she ever give the warmth of that hoarded up affection. And that lad was Ned Brady, the son of Peter Brady the hackler.

"Was that the priest's wee boy I saw at the door, Shelia?" asked the wheezy voice of a man who put his head into the McCann's kitchen. The girl started, almost upsetting the eggs she was trying to place neatly along the dresser, as if for exhibition.

"Oh, come on in Barney," the girl requested when she had steadied the eggs and seen who it was.

The man entered. Beholding the row of eggs he asked in surprise, "In the name of God where did ye get all the eggs?" then looking towards the window he asked, "Are ye thinking of starting a wee shop?" Sheila smiled. Satisfying herself that the eggs were secure in their position, she explained they were a present to her mother from Father Mick.

The visitor, Barney Bubbles Hanna the rougher, moved close to the dresser. With an amazed expression on his dust covered face he touched the eggs reverently.

"Man, its grand to think of a clergyman being so thoughtful." Then looking at the girl and knowing her poorly-fed mother was at her work he remarked: "That action's a damn sight better than all the sermon's he'll ever preach, and it'll be remembered a good sight longer."

"Will ye take a couple of them with ye for Mrs. Hanna?" the girl asked kindly, picking a few of the largest.

"By my soul, I'll do nothing of the kind," protested the rougher. "Do ye want me and them to be thrown out of the house? why it's giving ye something we should all be doing instead of taking from ye. Surely Sheila ye wouldn't insult me and mine to think we would deprive ye of one of them?"

Sheila was upset. She could not find words to reply whereupon, the rougher, with a hearty, "Much good may the priest's eggs do ye all!" left the house.

On his way down the street Barney Bubbles Hannah fingered in the pocket of his dirty torn coat until he had extracted a small, carefully wrapped parcel. It contained a quarter pound of fresh country butter he had bought that day from a country man, in order to give to the McCann's.

As he entered his own house and laid the small parcel on the kitchen table he murmured despondently to his wife, "It will do another time, it will do another time."

Because the tiny parcel had looked so small in comparison to the present from the priest, the big-hearted rougher had been ashamed to give it to the handsome girl.

CHAPTER FOUR

The Bradys

A few doors below Widow McCann's in Ravage's Row was where Peter Brady, the hackler, resided. As a boy Peter had come to Belfast with his father, mother, brothers and sisters. They had all heard the rattle of the linen town's machinery. The years had passed, his parents had died, the other members of the family scattered and Peter, now a fully qualified hackler, was a big man with a wife and son of his own.

When he had left Donegal, he was only nine years old, but he never forgot that departure. From a small plot of mountainy land overlooking the majestic Lough Swilly his parents and their children had been evicted. Bundled into a cart, that had been lent by a kindly neighbour, the evicted family had travelled via Derry to Belfast. On the journey his young eyes had seen humble cabins in flames, others being wrecked, and starved bodies of poor men, women and children laid out for burial along the road.

To his distracted father Belfast might have held out cruelties, but the poor man decided it could be no worse than Donegal where he had to listen to his little ones constantly crying for food. With his starving children, therefore, he had taken a chance and found his way to the town going mad on Linen. Years of agony in Donegal might be forgotten by years of agony in another place was how the tortured man may have thought. From his childhood he had been used to poverty and had long since become resigned to there being no heaven on earth for the worker.

In Belfast the evicted man soon found employment and as the mill-owners required young boys and girls his burden was somewhat eased by other members of the family also getting jobs. Although far away from the fresh purple hills of his beautiful native county the walls of the little home he secured in Ravage's Row began to ring with youthful laughter.

But the years passed and with them he and his wife died, to be followed by the breaking up of the family until the only member left in the old home in Ravage's Row was the son Peter. Peter got married and brought up a son whom he had christened Edward after an uncle, but as the same sounded to "toffy" for the neighbours it succumbed to Ned.

Peter Brady often recalled that early eviction of his parents and family and as his boyish eyes had seen red-coated soldiers in company with the evictors he always connected Red-coats with cruelty and with them associated all their allies. Thus, he looked upon the English and their friends as the cause of all the woes of the Irish people.

Being of a devout Catholic family he remembered his father had taught "to bear wrongs patiently and to forgive all injury" and that his parents could never see any possibility of relief from their conditions except through prayer. At heart, however, their son was a rebel, ever ready to fight against what he considered an injustice. In a short time he soon found plenty to protest against in his new surroundings but eventually learned that kicking in the traces of the system was hurtful to himself and also discovered he was frequently laughed at by other working-people who as Johnny Connor said, "Had licked the hands what flayed them." When he had "stood up to" a foreman or smashed a window to breath of fresh air into a suffocating hackling-shop or grumbled about the wages he was punished, and his wife and child missed his earnings until he was employed again.

As time went by Peter allied prayer to his struggle and became a model married man, working for God and drawing his wages from the mill-owners. Animated by a strong paternal passion he worked in the mills twelve hours each day with a determination to keep his wife and son outside them, actually stopping smoking and drinking completely in order that his boy might have a better chance in life than he had and studying what more he could possibly deny himself.

Adopting as headlines for his mode of living such sayings as "owe not any man" Peter, who was regarded as the bravest man in the Row, could face a bull but could not owe a penny.

In his ambition to keep his son and wife outside the mill, he succeeded. As the boy never entered the mill but became a clerk in one of the large offices in the town and his wife looked after the home.

His son Ned Brady was a splendid looking lad, a fine athlete, and as one of the neighbours said of him, "No son could have been more attached to his father and mother." Further he was cheery, loved life and loved the people of the mill-Rows.

About the time of the rougher Jimmy McCann's death Ned had reached his nineteenth year, and although poorly paid had, on account of his position, to dress somewhat better than the other lads of the Row who worked in the mills.

One evening, some months after the McCann's bereavement, Sheila their lovely daughter, was standing at the door as Ned Brady returned from his work in the town. To the lad's cheek there came a flush and his well-shaped legs wobbled on the paved footpath. Approaching he felt the girl's eyes on him and his steps grew staggerier as if he were drunk from the waist down. Something told him she was waiting for him. It was unusual for her to be outside when he was passing. When he reached her door, the girl reddened and extending her head forward almost whispered.

"I'm sorry, I can't see ye tonight Ned, my aunt's coming." Still unsteady but stammering "Alright," the lad without stopping passed down the street as Sheila went in and closed the door.

When he arrived home his tea was ready. Mrs. Brady danced attendance upon her son, but her lad was noticeably quiet at the table.

Since Sunday he had been looking forward to his walk with Sheila McCann and to say that he was disappointed would be to put it mildly. This walk was to have been their first walk together for although always admiring the girl at a distance and speaking to her in a passing Ned had never gathered sufficient courage to ask her for a walk until the previous Sunday. The poor boy had also been afraid she might refuse his invitation. Several lads he knew had asked and were turned down. When she consented to go with him, therefore, he felt he had secured the greatest victory anyone could wish in life. Since Sunday he had been counting the hours and looking forward so anxiously to his walk that he was battered down by her whispered: "I'm sorry I can't see ye tonight." To make things worse the night was a beautiful one and, on his way home he had been admiring the bright full moon that was lighting up the big dark hill.

Noticing her son's silence and thoughtfulness the attending mother anxiously enquired, "Is there anything a bother to ye, son? Is there anything on yer mind?"

Mrs. Brady's girlhood days had been spent on a farm, and she had conceived the idea that the headwork her son was called upon to do in an office was the hardest of all labours.

"No, ma, I'm alright," replied the quiet lad finishing his tea and staring through the short lace blinds on the window. The anxious mother was not going to be so easily dismissed however.

"Then what's weighing ye down, son?" she asked, beginning to clear the tea things away. "There's something bothering ye, because ye've hardly ate anything," then looking closer at her boy as she lifted the delph she feelingly asked, "Maybe ye're not feeling well, son - is that it?"

Remaining in the same position, his eyes fixed on the window, Ned answered, "No, Ma, I'm alright I tell ye."

"Then what makes ye so quiet and has ye staring out of the window that way?" persisted the mother, "It's not a bit like ye."

"There's nothing the matter with me, Ma, so don't be worrying yerself," the boy said assuringly, "I was just watching the girls skipping," as the thud, thud of the rope came from the street.

"Away and take a good long walk up the White Road to yerself," shouted a man's strong voice from the scullery as its owner, Ned's father, opened the door and came into the kitchen with his head and bare shoulders dripping with water. Rubbing himself with a towel, his vigour made one expect to see sparks.

"Man dear," he continued, "a fellow like you who's locked up inside at a desk all days needs all the fresh air he can get. Sling a lot of cold water over yerself, go away up to the hill, swing yer arms and breathe deep," he commanded smilingly, "and ye'll come back a new man."

"Nonsense, Peter" the mother protested, "It's rest and quiet in the house the boy's needing."

Ned could not help admiring the splendid shoulders and neck of his father as he watched him scrub them red with the towel, but his mind harboured his disappointed and Sheila's, "I can't see ye tonight" still rang in his ears.

"Don't heed yer Ma" boy continued the father, "she would make ye into a wee girl if she had her way. Pampering's only for oul' men and young women."

Then rubbing his chest wickedly, he barked out; "Put yer head below the tap, dry yerself well and go away up to the heather above Johnny Connor's and yer Ma won't know ye when ye come back."

In his seat the lad grew impatient and speaking towards the fireplace almost growled, "No, I'm not going out, I'm not going for any walk." Then turning towards his father he asked, "Don't ye think I've walked enough when I walked up from the town?"

Rubbing at his head the father laughed loudly. He was just in the act of answering when a gentle knock sounded at the door. Covering his naked chest with the towel the hackler retreated to the scullery.

When Mrs. Brady had opened the door, a little boy handed her a small slip of paper. "Ye're to give that to Ned", the boy said secretly. The mother took the paper from the child and saying "alright dear" closed the door.

"Who was that?" roared the voice of the father from the scullery when the door had been closed. "It's only one of the wee childer," quietly answered the mother.

"What do they want?" came again from the scullery.

"Nothing, nothing, yer fathers terrible nosey," the mother impatiently answered as she bent over the fire to poke it.

Peter became quiet. He had resigned himself and when all was silent the gentle mother leaned over and touched her son on the arm. Ned who was staring through the window turned round, with a finger at her lips his mother reached him the small bit of paper.

"One of the wee McCann's brought that for ye, son," she whispered.

Trying to appear unconcerned the boy took it. The mother crossed the kitchen and disappeared up the stairs.

"Where are ye goin'?" asked the voice from the scullery, as her feet fell on the stairs.

"To make the beds," was the reply.

Excitedly Ned Brady unfolded the piece of paper and on it read, "Aunt Margaret cannot come so I can, Sheila."

The thud, thud of the rope outside was drowned in the thump, thump of the lad's heart. Folding up the sacred message and hiding it away in his vest pocket, he jumped from his chair and rushed towards the scullery just as his father was coming out.

"Where are ye going now?" asked the father, almost knocked off his feet by the son's haste.

With his handsome face beaming with smiles the lad replied pleasantly, "I'm taking yer advice, da, I'm going to throw plenty of cowl water on myself and take a long walk over the hill", adding coyly, "it should do me a world of good."

Peter Brady looked at his fine boy with pride and surprise. Humorously grunting, "Ye're a great fellow," he passed through the kitchen and calling, "Have ye a shirt for me up there?" to his wife and proceeded upstairs.

In the room where the mother was tidying up, he asked in a low voice, "Maggie was that one of the wee McCann's that was at the door a while ago?"

"It was, Peter," the wife replied somewhat reluctantly, "why do ye ask?" she questioned, continuing with her tidying.

"I just thought so," hummed Peter, pulling at his braces on the end of the bed and beginning to sing "I wander today to the hills, Maggie to watch the scenes below."

CHAPTER FIVE

Ned and Sheila

Peter Brady and his wife Maggie remained upstairs while the splash, splash of water sounded from the scullery and until the opening and closing of the front door told them their boy had gone for his walk. As the pat, pat of his brisk steps sounded on the street outside they came quietly down to the kitchen.

Passing the McCann's home, the young man felt his heartbeat so loud that he closed his eyes in an effort to prevent it being heard inside the girls' house while the "Hellos" from the neighbours added to his embarrassment. At the top of the street, he did not dare to look back to see if the girl were coming, but swerving quickly to the right proceeded up the steep road towards the dark mountain, all the time fancying he heard the rhythm of her footsteps coming behind, when in reality, it was only the thumping of his own heart.

Walking on until he had reached the big clump of trees at the Ardoyne corner, he stopped to wait. Although sorely tempted to look down the road he resisted and instead fixed his eyes on the big broad hill before him. At no time, he thought, had the Dark Hill looked more beautiful. In the light of a cloudless moon and against an amber sky its graceful curves seemed to make his head grow dizzy until a passing voice said playfully, "Behold the Princess comes."

With a shake he awoke himself from his reverie and turned from the hill in time to receive a passing wink from Barney Bubbles the rougher, and to discover that Sheila McCann was almost beside him.

"I'm sorry for keeping ye waiting," the girl breathlessly began, "but I hurried all I could when I saw ya passing the window." Then she looked down and blushed.

The rougher's passing remark and the girl's sudden arrival had the young man confused. Sheila's voice appeared to be far away. The dark hill seemed to have laid a pulling hand upon his shoulder. He wanted to rush with the girl to its heathery top.

A swift glance told him that Sheila's face was radiant and her dress becoming, but without opening his mouth to speak he strode across the road with his breathless companion trotting beside him. As if stimulated by the girl's presence and the hill's attraction his vigorous strides made it difficult for her to keep up with him.

"Aunt Margaret couldn't come tonight so I was able to get out but she's coming up to our house tomorrow night."

Walking with his eyes on the ground, he nodded his head. For him it was enough just then to hear her voice, words didn't matter. As she talked, he strode on with pressed lips.

"She sent word with Pat O'Neill, the car man that she couldn't come. Pat takes her for drives since she came from America and today he had her at Holywood."

The girl was breathing fast. Discovering that he was walking too quickly Ned shortened his stride but said nothing.

Panting the girl went on. "We were down to see her at her hotel last night. My ma and me. She must have plenty of money Ned the way she goes about and lives."

Her companion nodded and although now almost breathless the girl resumed.

"She knew yer da, Ned, before she went to America," then with a smile and an effort to look up into her companion's face, "she says she was an oul' girl of his before yer ma got him, but she says he got the finest girl in the whole town."

The young man just grunted, the girl bubbling with talk trotted beside him. "She says yer da was the best Irishman the district had in the oul' days and that he was a great friend of the priests and could fight or run any man in the country."

"Oh Ned" she added with deliberation, "ye should hear her sing yer da's praises, I believe she's in love with him yet."

Ned shook his head, but content to listen to the musical voice and pit-pat of the little feet marched on without replying. Along the road he raised his eyes to look at the dark hill which, drew nearer and nearer while the girl continued talking and her cheery chatter was all about what her Aunt Margaret had said of his father. How she had seen him throw shoulderstone, and bullets, play draughts, run races, hold the hand-ball alley, fight and lead the marching Nationalists in procession, and how all the girls had loved him in the old days. Pleased to hear the praises of the father to whom he was so attached and particularly when they came from such beautiful lips as Sheila's, he plodded on in silence and pride.

"She says he was always the life and soul of the district when she lived here and that he will never be forgotten by his old friends."

Awakening to the fact that the girl was almost gasping with walking, talking and enthusiasm, Ned again shortened his strides. For a few steps Sheila was silent, as if waiting for a word from her companion, but none came.

"Does yer da ever talk of the early days, Ned?" she then asked and again waited.

"He does very often," was all the reply.

"Aunt Margaret says he was a very smart man and that it was a pity to see him a hackler."

"That's what I think too," Ned replied sharply, adding with a tinge of bitterness and determination in his voice.

"It had always been my ambition to work hard and make enough money so that he can leave the filthy mills."

The tone of his voice shocked Sheila who immediately lapsed into silence as she felt his anger. His remark had chased the action from her lips to the inside of her pretty head. Her eyes dimmed and instead of looking up at his face they searched the ground. The bubbling ceased and for some time the young pair walked along in silence.

The steep white road that lost itself in the heather of the dark hill stretched before them. From each side the green bushes strove to kiss above their heads. The girl took one side of the road, the boy the other. The long white ribbon of limestone lay between and before them. On they walked. The hilltop drew nearer and the evening's growing silence weighed heavily with their own.

Flap, flap came the sudden gentle noise of a bird that flew from where the girl passed. Sufficient to startle her she watched it fly across the road to where bursting into song it gave life to the branch of an old dead tree. Almost as quickly as the bird, Sheila flew across to her companion, and dreading that her voice might disturb the song, softly asked, "What kind of a bird is that Ned?" Then pointing to the tree, she whispered, "See there it is. Isn't its song beautiful?"

The young man brightened up. He loved to talk of birds and flowers and trees and fields. "That's a robin," he proudly explained while the girl drew closer to him and began plying him with questions about the things she noticed on the way.

He answered question after question and then continued pointing out the spots where, as a schoolboy, he used to gather haws for the pluffers he made from the stalks of the colts foot in the quarry and where he strung blackberries on a straw, made cages from rushes for butterflies, and also made Saint Bridge's crosses, to bring home to his mother. Sheila had also gathered flowers and blackberries on the hill and recalled how her father used to take her with him to get whin blossoms to dye the eggs yellow for the children at Easter.

"He's a nice little fellow but he can be a wee brute when he likes," the young man remarked on hearing another robin on the way but the girl did not want to hear of brutes that evening and quickly replied, "He's a beautiful singer," as they passed the bird, Ned looked up and quietly remarked, "He sings very well but not near as well as the lark, wait until you get to the top of the hill and hear the larks."

Continuing their climb, a long conversation about birds took place, Sheila asking her questions and her hero gladly supplying the answers. Until then, Ned Brady never realised his interest in birds could be so valuable. So absorbed were they that the steepness of the rough white road was forgotten, and they reached the top before they realised it.

"Hello childer." The voice of Johnny Connor the hillman reached them. He had seen the two young people from the town approach as he leaned across the half-door of his cabin and hurrying forward to meet them, he shook hands warmly with the girl, sympathetically remarking.

"I was terrible sorry about the death of yer poor father. God rest him, he was a good soul if ever there was one but sure he's only away a wee while before the rest of us."

The girl lowered her head and her rosy lips paled. Without raising her eyes, she thanked the hillman.

"He loved this place of yours Johnny and he loved the heather." She said as she raised her eyes to look around.

"Poor soul he did that. When he was any way half at himself, he always struggled up here on a Sunday. Poor man, to serve his family he made a powerful effort to keep what little life he had in his body, but the dammed mills and the long hours were too many for him." The girl sobbed, as the hillman continued. "Manys the crack the two of us had up here," and pointing to the spring well near the house, "manys a drink yer father took out of the oul' well and thought it was giving him new life."

"He was very fond of you, Johnny," sighed the girl.

"No fonder than I was of him," was the prompt reply. "Yer father was a kindly good man and if he had any fault at all it was that he loved his wife and childer so well he was continually worried by the dread of them having to live as he had lived. But tell me girl," he asked, "how is yer mother bearing up?"

"My ma is working every day," the girl replied adding, Johnny thought, with sorrow in her voice, "And Aunt Margaret is going to take me out to America next week. So that I may get work out there and be able to send money home to keep my ma and the childer."

Ned Brady shuffled his feet and coughed.

"So, I heard girl. There'll be more missing ye than yer mother," smiled the hillman, squinting at the young man who had walked away towards the end of the house, where, with a solemn face, he stood staring at the mills below.

Touching her wet eyes and looking after the young Brady, Sheila whispered, "He'll soon forget me Johnny, he'll soon forget me."

The hillman assumed a fatherly attitude. Placing a hand on the girl's shoulder he consoled her. "Oh, no, if he's anything like his own father he'll not forget ye. His father's good stuff and it should be in the son. There never was anybody around the mills could hold a candle to Peter Brady and if I'm a judge, at all, that lad of his is a chip of the oul' block."

"Out of sight's out of mind Johnny," the girl replied, brightening, but the mountainy man knew how she was thinking and quickly answered, "That wasn't so with oul' Kate Gillen and Paddy Ryan."

The girl knew this old couple well. They lived in a big parlour house not far from the Row and were nicknamed, Darby and Joan.

"Over fifty years ago Paddy kissed Kate goodbye," began Johnny. "Paddy went to America to push his fortune and wandered to the far west. Soon after he sent her three letters, but the third was the last to come. The years passed. Kate's mother, father and sister died, and she grew old and lived alone. The neighbours were kind and gave her oul' fingers wee bits of sewing and darning to do. That and charity kept her alive, but the workhouse was approaching. Then one day a cablegram came from across the seas. It was from Paddy, - after over forty years. At last a lucky stroke had made him rich and although very oul' he wanted his oul' sweetheart to come to him. Illness and misfortune had dogged him up till then. Well, Kate went out to her oul' boy. They got married. He sold his property, they came back here made a home, and now down at the mills they call them Darby and Joan."

Johnny stopped, then rubbing his head with his rough hand he looked admiringly at the straight silent figure of Peter Brady's fine son outlined against a background of dark heather. A gentle squeeze of gratitude on his arm, a soft thankful voice saying, "Oh. Jonny, I never heard that before," and hurrying feet told the mountainy man that Sheila was off to the boy and as he heard her race he smiled.

The two young people soon found a spot among the heather that looked inviting, and both sat down. Sheila, still burned from Johnny's story. With face flushed by enthusiasm she unfolded it to Ned Brady who, as he listened, found nothing but torture in the thoughts of the long separation of poor Paddy and Kate. Unaware of this the girl talked and talked. Her boy pulled wickedly at the heather around them. When she had finished there was silence. With his eyes looking out towards the east Ned fingered the heather. Like a shawl the quietness of the hill seemed to wrap itself around the pair. She moved closer to the lad. For some minutes they remained thus, the girl, as it were, peeping out of her shawl of silence to await the boy's voice, but with his eyes riveted on something far away Ned sat silent.

"What are ya looking at, Ned?" his companion at last asked casting away from her mystic shawl and playfully tickling one of his ears with a long grass. The lad smiled and shook his head.

"Yonder is McArt's fort. Look how plain it is," he explained dreamily, "that's where the United Irishmen once held up their hands and swore to free their country." he sighed. "If only they had been able to lift the torture from the poor people!"

Sheila slid nearer to watch his brightening eyes. On no subject did Ned Brady warm so much as that of his country and its people. When he spoke of their wrongs, he was the enraged warrior.

'How manly and noble he looked,' she thought silencing

her breathing lest it should disturb him. Her eyes feasted on his handsome young face. He was very like his father, - she decided. Still gazing towards the far away fort he rambled on.

"That hill has a strange history of kings and robbers. Cormac McArt used to sit in judgement there and in later years pirates frequented its caves. Those were the men who didn't work and ruled. Now one wonders will the working people themselves ever rule. Today they are ruled by different kinds of exploiters all of whom are little kings in their own way. They continue slaving the working people while they enjoy the luxury the slavery provides - and crack their whips for more."

As he spoke, his face lit up and his chin moved forward. Sheila sat breathless and happy, watching and listening to the warm words that fell like torrents from his lips.

Sitting thus on the scented heather, the dark hill towering above, the deep valley stretching towards the town below, the snug white cottage close by, the changing amber sky over all and hearing the sound of a fresh manly musical voice and the song of the larks the girl's eyes wandered towards the sky. How near, she thought, it was to heaven - to be up beside Johnny Connor's cabin. No wonder than people in the mill rows spoke of it as Next Stop Heaven.

A man's voice was singing on a pad below them in the whins. The young pair could hear the words *'The green grove has gone from the hill Maggie, where first the daisies spring'.*

"Hello, hello there, young people!" shouted the man's strong voice, as its owner, swinging his arms with a military air jogged merrily down the rough hill. The young couple were surprised. Looking in the direction of the voice they beheld Ned's father as he was fast disappearing behind the row of hedges that skirted the road. For some time, they sat and listened till the song had died away.

Having been taken by surprise the boy and girl were unable to speak but looking into each other's eyes they sighed and then burst out laughing. To be discovered by his father was a bit of a shock for Ned who later learned that Johnny Connor, had seen the elder Brady approach and had called and whistled to them in vain.

CHAPTER SIX

Barney Bubbles Hanna, the Rougher

After passing his son and the girl McCann, Peter Brady, with a mixture of thoughts, swung down the dark hill. He had heard the young girl was going to America and was sorry, not only for his boy's sake but also for hers, because he knew she did not want to leave home. Her departure, he realised would pain his son, but understandingly the lad he knew if the girl remained true to him he would be true to her, and he could think of no better partner for his boy. They were both young and had the world before them and they were neighbours' children.

Discovering the boy and girl sitting like a pair of young birds amongst the heather on the hill had brought back the memory of other days. With a thrilling joy the big hackler had recalled the time when he used to drag his own sweetheart Maggie from the dull streets of the town and find romance and happiness on the same spot above Johnny Connor's cabin home. Today that sweetheart was the lad's mother and the years, having told their tale upon her, had left her no longer able to join her sturdy husband on his long rambles up the steep hill.

Alone, however, Peter Brady continued to visit the favourite old haunts. Each time, with a bunch of heather, he carried back memories to the old home. To see and handle the purple bloom was now almost as good as the walk to Mrs. Brady. At least so she said.

Long walks, fresh air, and cold water were her husband's cures for almost anything, and his programme for a ramble generally included, admiring the scenery, taking deep breathes, swinging the arms, singing songs, reciting a few verses, making a speech to the hedges, having a long drink of spring water, eating a handful of dandelions and chanting some prayers. As with chest expanded, he marched along the country roads one could hear him say with thankfulness. "It's a great change from the stuffy oul' hackling shop."

After passing the young couple on the hill, Peter had walked about half-way down the steep white road trying by prayer to induce God to ease his daily burden and the burdens of others, when he heard a cough from someone on the ditch by the side of the road. He knew its owner. There was only one such cough.

"My God is it you Barney Bubbles?" he exclaimed, halting and addressing Barney Bubbles Hanna the rougher who, noted for his bad chest, was lying resting on his back on the ditch. To all and sundry the rougher was known as Barney Bubbles because of the amusing habit he had of always flipping bright little bubbles from the tip of his tongue.

"My God, have ye been able to get up this far?" the hackler asked again in surprise.

The wheezy voice coughed, and its owner sat up.

"I just had to, Peter. The wife doesn't know I'm up here at all, but I couldn't help it. I wanted to struggle up as far as Johnny Connor's, but the braes beat me, I haven't the wind."

With compassion the hackler looked at his fellow-worker. Both men were about the same age, came from the same county, had been neighbours' children, and were now neighbours in Ravages Row. Barney Bubbles, Peter thought, had always been too fond of spending his spare time and spare money in public-houses and so his ruined lungs were now craving for fresh air. On account of the nature of his work the hackler always dreaded lung trouble. Gazing critically at his friend and hearing his wrecking cough he was convinced his days of climbing up the steep hill to Johnny Connor's cabin were near an end. To Peter Brady life without that climb would not be worth living. Next to a visit to the church the walk to the hill was his greatest consolation. Full of sympathy, therefore, he sat down on the green ditch beside his weary neighbour.

"Are ye not getting any more rest from the cough?" he asked anxiously.

Through wheezes and coughs Barney Bubbles answered, "Man, Peter I've tried everything to get ease from it but not the bit of good it is," then after waiting for a fit to subside he added breathlessly, "I'm thinking the blasted thing's come to take me this time, right enough, but to tell ye the truth I'm worrying more about my work than about it."

"What," he asked tearfully, "would the wife and childher, God help them, do if I had to cave in now Peter?" Poor Jimmy McCann, God help him can hardly rest in his grave. I'm sure for thinking of the way he left his wife and childer."

"Maybe now that the summer is here ye'll feel a lot better," said his friend consolingly.

"Ah, no, Peter," lamented the sick man, "ye know yerself that it's worse it does be in the shop in the hot weather when there's bad flax and bad ventilation and damn all I seem to get but bad flax and we always have bad ventilation." His friend's face grew cloudy.

"That's true" he agreed, "some of the confounded owners wouldn't let a breath of air in for fear it would injure a parcel of flax and they don't care a jot what harm it does a worker, we're less important than their flax or their machines Barney. Take plenty of fresh air," urged Peter. "Take plenty of fresh air it costs nothing."

The rougher coughed. "Man dear, I be that tired," he groaned, "when I get out of the blooming mill that I haven't the heart or legs to move any further than the end of the street."

To Barney Bubbles as to the other workers the dread of the sack always loomed large and terrorizing. With it the poor man saw his home lost and his wife and children starving. Fast failing health stood between him and that. If it collapsed completely all collapsed with it. "It's the spirit he has that keeps him up," many neighbours said of him.

"For heaven's sake man try and get as much fresh air as ye can Barney, and don't be too anxious about yer work, it'll be alright," said Peter assuringly.

The weary man spat out, "No, no, Peter. Ye don't know our foreman. He's like one of the owner's machines. He forgets he was a rougher once himself and forgets we're only human beings. Last week he groused at me. We were working on Irish flax and terrible hard stuff it is to work. If only we were on to Belgian, I wouldn't be half as bad as I am. I always be worse with the Irish and the foreman told me if I didn't stop my barking and speed up I'd have to get out, I was in one of those awful kinks I take."

"He's just like all the rest of the bosses' men," snapped the hackler bitterly, "does he never think of the forty years ye've slaved for the firm? The curse of God's on them and their grinding, Barney and there'll be a day of reckoning for it all yet. No wonder Johnny Connor up on the hill says, we're just like butter, and the price that's ruling the market is all that's paid for us to grease their machinery, we're just grease for their machines. Even the young priest, Father Mick, says that a few piles of stones are all that's left of the landed civilizations of Egypt and Babylon because even in those days the working people were treated just like dirt, and I heard Johnny Connor say, *'The people will eventually vomit those who are destroying them'.*

The sick man brightened up with Peter's speech. He loved his big friend, admired his strength, applauded his courage, valued his friendship, and even liked to quarrel with him occasionally.

Clearing his throat, he began: "When I was younger, Peter, I didn't mind the work nor the hours at all but now it's different, the work gets very, very hard and the hours terrible, terrible long as ye get older and weaker. "Mind yer health Peter," he enjoined "For God's sake mind yer health," as a fit of coughing seized him.

Rising from the ditch the hackler smiled, "Leave it to

me, Barney. That's my disease. The wife says I look after myself so well it'll kill me. Ye should hear her sometimes telling me I'll wash the head and walk the legs off myself and blow my lungs out with air sometime till they burst."

Joining in the smile the rougher stifled another cough and got up from his seat. "Mrs. Brady's like my own oul' woman, she doesn't mean half of what she says, ye know Peter if ye heeded a woman at all ye couldn't live with her."

The two men set out on their walk homewards while the rougher continued, "Yer wife always has a quiet bid in her and suffers most from her fondness for you. She's a grand soul, yer wee woman, Peter. God knows what the street would do without her. Every man and woman and child that's sick think they can't get well if she's not with them. Why my oul' woman says she's better than all the doctors and nurses put together and Peter many's a terrible bill she saved a lot of us."

Peter Brady loved to hear the praises of his gentle wife and listening to his friend, the two workmen proceeded down the white road just as young Ned Brady and Sheila McCann came out from a lane behind them. Recognising the figures in front the lad pulled the girl back to the bushes where they remained until the elder men had gone completely out of sight.

On the sloping road Barney Bubbles footsteps were uncertain and his progress slow. Peter was therefore forced to slacken his usual pace and occasionally stop until spasms of his friend's cough had abated. At one of these rests he remarked, "Man Barney, ye're a far changed man from the time ye and me used to run the races."

A new light came into the rougher's eyes. "Ah, them were the grand oul' days, Peter," he said enthusiastically resuming the walk.

"Man, dear there was very few could lick ye then at fighting, running or walking," Peter reminded.

"Ye weren't bad stuff yerself," The rougher's head was high.

His friend smiling pleasantly, "I remember ye walloping the Scotch half-mile champion, Barney, on the Antrim Road and saw ya being carried home shoulder high."

Barney's step grew brisker and his cough disappeared. "Ah that was a tough tussle. Do ye mind I made a burst in the first quarter and the Scotch fellow was taken so completely by surprise that he couldn't wipe away the lead I got." A new colour had come to the sick man's face and his steps became so brisk that his friend was obliged to increase his stride.

"Ye had a fine record at the bullets too," said Peter thoughtfully, his mind rummaging in the past, "I remember ye whacking all before ye round the Horse Shoe Line when ye were hardly more than twenty-one."

"Ye mean in the big County Match." Bubbles stuck his chest out. He began breathing deeply and striding step for step alongside the big hackler.

"I had to fight every inch of the way that day Peter. It was a stiff contest but d'ye mind I gained the head by a trick swing at a bend of the road and never lost it again."

By this time the rougher was a step or two ahead of

his companion so that the latter had to move even more quickly in order to keep abreast. Barney was striding out like a young fellow and his cough was forgotten. "There was some excitement in the Row that night."

"Ha, Ha," laughed Barney "and ye made a tremendous speech about Ireland and hurt some people's feelings in yer enthusiasm."

"The hackler frowned. Then he joined his friend in the laughter that followed. "I remember that night only too well. As a result of what I said I had to fight Billy Johnston after it, and got a fine black eye for my trouble."

Laughing heartily both men turned the Ardoyne corner where coming into the sight of the high mills the subject changed.

As Peter saw that huge buildings towering before them, he remarked, "There's plenty of work in Ritchell's Mill this weather."

The rougher's cough suddenly came back. With a subdued voice he asked, "Is that so?" His step weakened; his eyes darkened. The hackler who persisted in talking about work was obliged to slacken his pace. The very appearance of the big mills and mention of work had had their effect. The rougher's spirit sank. The grand old days that stirred him so had disappeared. Monday morning and all it meant was coming. With feet that dragged heavily after him and a cough that lengthened as he drew nearer the poor man at last arrived in Ravage's Row with his sturdy friend and was glad when he reached a chair in his own kitchen, where he had to sit coughing and listening to his wife reprimanding him for trying to climb hills at his time of life and with the cough bad on him.

CHAPTER SEVEN

A Birth in The Row

Maggie the wife of Peter Brady was a small, quiet, gentle woman. She was of a race of slaving mothers. When her man and son were in the home, she served them untiringly. When they were out, amidst preparing for their return, she continually prayed for them. If you had asked her why she prayed the poor woman would probably have told you it was because she felt closer to them in prayer. Her prayers she also believed helped and protected them. More than a hundred times a day the small kitchen house in Ravage's Row heard her pleading, "God bless my Peter and my Ned, God bless everybody." By the neighbours she was called an angel, not because of her prayers but because of her kindness, and the neighbours knew. For a definition of "an angel" you might have been informed that it was, "one who could forget herself in another's trouble," and Mrs. Brady was that and more.

When she was nineteen years old, she had married Peter. From the country near Downpatrick where she had been the only girl in a poor but large family occupying a very small farm, she had to come to Belfast. Thinking her beauty of heart and form entitled her to something better than a miserable existence on the land and having foolish notions about the town, her brothers had sent her to learn dressmaking and grow up a lady. She was too good to ever grow into the kind of lady, then the popular and the handsome hackler soon ended her apprenticeship to the dressmaking. Having made the acquaintance of the lovely fresh young girl soon after her arrival, the dashing young hackler courted her for a few months and then they were married.

Before she had time to look around her, Maggie McCartan, as Maggie Brady, was imprisoned in a small kitchen house in Ravage's Row and after that she never had an opportunity. Having seen nothing but slavery and poverty in the area from which she had come and having experienced no better she made a perfect slave. Like thousands of others she resigned herself to her servitude accepting it as a purgatorial step to heaven, while Peter, her husband hackled flax for God, got his wages from the Mill-owners and continued to bark at the cruelties surrounding them.

On the Saturday evening that the son and Sheila McCann had been hailed on the dark, green, hill by the father, a birth had thrilled Ravage's Row and Mrs. Brady had been called to lend a hand. When all was over and the little one bathed the "angel", the woman hurried back home to prepare the tea for her son and husband. She was thus engaged when the sister of the proud mother dropped into thank her for all the good service she had rendered. In the district no birth ever passed without a treat, so, when the woman closed the door and satisfied herself that nobody else was in the house, her hand disappeared deep down beneath her shawl and reappeared holding a bottle.

"It's just a wee mouthful for our two selves and I want to thank ye for all yer trouble," said the woman scanning the dresser for a cup she soon discovered.

It was evident Mrs. Brady was uncomfortable. Before she had left the birth chamber, she had drank to the baby's health quite generously and was still feeling the effects of it.

"Thank ye, thank ye all the same, but I couldn't possibly take another drop" she pleaded nervously, but the woman would take no refusal.

"Stuff and nonsense, it will do ye a world of good," pouring a good glass into the cup and reaching it to the excited woman, "sure ye couldn't refuse a treat on an occasion like this. Our Sarah doesn't often give us a lift. Why Barney Bubbles says the only good thing she ever done was having this baby and he knows her for he used to do a line with her himself."

Mrs. Brady demurred, but the cup was pushed into her hand. "Swallow it woman, ye need it, it will do ye a lot of good. I go it in Lisa's and it's a wee drop of special."

Peter's wife surrendered. Staring towards the window she wished good health and long life to the mother and child as she drank quickly.

"My man Peter death on drink," she explained, starting on hearing a noise in the street. "Everybody knows that about him and well seen on him for it," said the woman. "Sure, everybody knows your Peter hates drink that much he wouldn't speak to a publican, but," she added, "he'll never be a bit the wiser of it."

"Ye know," Mrs. Brady explained, "Peter never took drink nor smoked from the time our son Ned was born and he wouldn't allow spirits into the house at any time since."

"A wee drop at a time like this doesn't do a body any harm," replied the woman eyeing the bottle as her nervous friend eyed the window.

Mrs. Brady was shaking. She feared the arrival of her husband. "Feth no" she stammered, "but my face gets a kind of flushed with it and I be terrible nervous of Peter noticing the drop on me."

"Don't worry about him, its special," drawled the woman. The visitor began to fumble again with the bottle and before the distracted woman had time to realise it another drink was poured into the cup. This discovery added to her confusion but seeing it was useless to protest she swallowed the whiskey hurriedly and began pleading as she looked at the clock.

"Oh, please run home now, my Peter's very punctual and he'll be here at any minute."

The visitor drank her whiskey and looking at the clock placed her empty cup on the dresser and began tucking her shawl around her. "Indeed, I'll better be hurrying myself Mrs. Brady for my man has no patience at all at the mealtimes and he's due very soon." Preparing to go she wiped her mouth with her hand while Mrs. Brady hid the cups in the scullery and returned fixing her hair. "Do ye think Peter would notice the wee drop on me?" she asked anxiously. At the moment heavy steps sounded on the street. "Run, run for God's sake run by the back," the muddled soul called excitedly, as the tall figure of her husband passed by the kitchen window.

Shoving the bottle beneath her blouse the visitor rushed through the scullery and escaped by the back as the hackler opened the door and entered the kitchen. In a second his distracted wife had taken up a bending position near the fire where with the poker she had begun to clear the grate. She looked guilty.

"I would have been back earlier only for falling in with Barney Bubbles on the White Road. Taking off his coat glanced at his wife, the clock, the table, and passing into the scullery where he turned on the tap, splashed the cold water over his face and began singing "and now we are aged and grey, Maggie, and the trials of life nearly done." While her husband was thus engaged Mrs. Brady tremblingly prepared his tea, at the same time struggling to prevent the woman's treat from overcoming her. Her face was flushed and her hands unsteady. "Barney Bubbles cough is worse than ever," shouted the voice from the scullery between splashes. "His chest wouldn't have troubled him if he had spent more of his time in the fresh air and less of it in the public-house, he was always a fool that way," his wife shivered uneasily. Pursuing her work silently she heard the splash, splash and song continued until her man scrubbing his face with a rough towel, came back into the kitchen...

"The pubs have knocked about twenty years off Bubbles' life and what health he has now isn't worth having at all. Drink's the curse of God and the ruination of the working people," he roared angrily as he rubbed.

A cup, falling from the woman's trembling hands, smashed on the tiled floor. The hackler stopped scrubbing, flinging the towel on a chair he asked anxiously. "What's happened?" Then without waiting for an answer he knelt down and began gathering up the pieces at the same time commanding, "Watch Maggie and don't cut yer fingers." As the wife, in a stupid kind of way, was also grabbing here and there at the bits of delph. "It's newens for you to smash anything girl," the big man said kindly, side glancing at his wife. "I'm not feeling a bit too well Peter, the birth has me all upset," Mrs. Brady explained.

"Not a bit of wonder. Ye've yerself killed attending to the neighbours. That birth up the street has taken more out of you that out of the woman who had the little one. It's a rest ye need. Go on up to bed and lie down for a while. It's a good rest ye need."

This suggestion relieved the poor woman who just then required no further advice. Consoling herself with the thought that her husband had not detected her condition and dreading that she might get worse from the effects of the drink she quietly retreated upstairs where she lay down on her bed.

Her husband had almost finished his tea when his son, Ned arrived home. Throwing his cap on the top of the dresser, the lad sat down in his usual place at the table. Looking round the kitchen he asked, "Where's ma?" To which the father answered, "she's gone upstairs to lie down for a wee while, don't be shouting." His mother's absence at meal-hours was so unusual that the lad fearing something serious had happened looked worried. "Is she ill?" he asked, "is ma ill?"

Smilingly rising from the table, the father placed his hand

on his son's head and whispered in this ear. "Don't worry lad, she's alright. There was a birth up the street and some o' the well-meaning women must have given her a wee drop too much." Then putting his fingers to his lips, he added, "But of course lad, mum's the word, for God's sake never let her know that I noticed it at all."

CHAPTER EIGHT

Sunday

T here were no rappers-up in Ravage's Row on Sunday morning and no screaming horns. Every other day was heralded by fiendish noises. As early as 4.30am, the rappers-up began their hammering of windows and doors. From five o'clock the mill-horns commenced screaming and hurrying feet rattled along the street.

Barney Bubbles, who did not sleep well with the coughing would have told you the two hours each morning before the mills started at 6.30 were "hell let loose" and that is was "pleasanter to get up than lie on". Poor Barney like the older folk, had, in his childhood days, been awakened by the songs of the birds. All of the old residenters had come in from the country and in the mills' din it was not easy for them to forget it. For them comparison was painful but their children, having had been born in the mill Rows knew no better.

On Sunday morning, there was a change of prologue. Except for the music of the church bell all was quiet. Encouraged as it were by the peacefulness more wild birds than usual came down from the hills to pay a fleeting visit to the Row and to give pleasure to the eyes that watched in wonderment through the small kitchen windows. To coax the visitors back the older folk scattered crumbs around the door and told the children of the lovely birds that used to visit their early country homes. The wild birds brought remembrance. Old and young in the Row loved Sunday. To the little ones it brought freedom from school and to the others a rest from rent-men, tick-men, shopkeepers' boys and slavery. No wonder the workers thought of God. Many of them took a long lie in bed but Peter Brady was so well drilled to jumping our early that he could not stay any longer on a Sunday. He had more time to sing and splash cold water over himself, so he took the fullest advantage of the day of freedom and went to early mass. But, early though he rose, he was always preceded by his wife.

"I'm tramped to pieces by that woman," he used to jokingly say, for Mrs. Brady tramped over him getting out of bed each morning and tramped over him again getting back each night. In their home she was always first to rise and last to retire.

Sunday morning was no exception, so Mrs. Brady went to the same mass as her husband. Their son, Ned, however, was more modern. He lay longer than usual but always managed somehow to scramble out in them for the ten o'clock service.

On the Sunday preceding Sheila McCann's departure for America, Mrs. McCann, the bereaved widow and Barney Bubbles Hanna's wife, in their black shawls, sneaked up the road to ten o'clock mass together. On the way young Ned Brady, dressed as they said, "like a new pin", passed them, but though the lad looked in their direction and called "Hello" the women merely tightened their shawls around their faces and did not reply. He was too well dressed to speak to, they thought. Very few well-dressed people wanted to speak to or be spoken to by women with shawls particularly on a leading thoroughfare and, forby, Ned Brady worked now amongst the well-off people in the town. It might do to speak to him in the Row but outside it was different.

When the lad had passed, Mrs. Hanna, whose eyes followed his stately figure, whispered through her shawl, "Isn't Ned Brady getting terrible like his da?"

"Ne is that," the widow, also watching the splendid form stride up the hill before her, agreed.

"He'll be a fine young man for whoever gets him and it's a terrible pity yer girl Sheila is going to America for I think he likes her," said Mrs. Hanna tucking at her shawl.

"Poor Sheila," lamented the widow, "I think it will go very hard with her leaving the Row. She has a great affection for that boy of Peter Brady's. Poor thing she cried very sore in the room last night."

"It'll be harder on her than the death of her da," Mrs. Hanna remarked knowingly, "for I can mind how my own sister Bella was when she left her fellow to go to America twenty years ago and it just after my da died."

Continuing their conversation, the two women finished their short journey up the road and reached the steps leading to the church.

"It's Father Mick that's on the door this morning," whispered Mrs. McCann, looking cautiously and then pulling the shawl down over most of their face.

"There's a big difference between him and Father Alexander," came the muffled reply from below the other shawl as the two women drew closer together.

"Feth aye," almost breathed Mrs. McCann, "Father Mick speaks to everybody, but Father Alexander only smiles at them that has something. God Bless Father Mick he would speak to ye even in the town and ye with a shawl on ye."

"They say Father Mick's own people are just as poor as we are; maybe that accounts for it," Mrs. Hanna explained. Moving silently up the steps and keeping close to the side with the overhanging bushes the two women continued whispering. At the top Father Mick stood engaged in conversation with a little boy. "We'll be able to juke by without being seen," whispered Mrs. Hanna but as the shawl covered figures with their faces well-hidden sneaked past him the young priest spoke.

"Is that you Mrs. McCann?" he called to the women's embarrassment. They stopped. The young priest came forward and asked about their families after which, he gave each of them an affectionate pat on the head telling them to say a prayer for him when they got inside. Happy at being "made of" they left his reverence, they released their shawls to expose more of their faces and passed proudly into the church, where in the side chapel they found a secluded spot near the wall.

On a Sunday all the early services were thronged by the shawled people, but at the last mass (12 o'clock) few came, it being mainly attended by the "toffy" people from the town who had to work less and could sleep more. Such fortunate folk were not expected to upset their usual routine even on a Sunday.

Ten o'clock mass to which the two women had come was the Children's mass. All the little ones from the Mill Rows attended it and filled the centre seats. The building being cruciform, older people occupied the small side chapels.

As soon as Mrs. Hanna and Mrs. McCann had reached their places of one of the side chapels, the service commenced, and the children's fresh young voices filled the artistically decorated building with an opening hymn. With hands tightly clasped and eyes fixed on the flower-decked altar the widow McCann prayed for the soul of her late husband and for a safe journey to America for her daughter Sheila. While she was thus engaged her friend Mrs. Hanna was asking God to relieve her husband's cough and help him to keep his job in the Roughing-shop.

On the far side of the church, with head bowed and a chew of tobacco in his mouth to keep him from coughing Barney Bubbles himself, was imploring Jesus to watch over his wife and children in case anything should happen to him and asking St Patrick to send Belgian flax to the mills instead of Irish, while in a seat in front Johnny Connor from the dark hill was fervently praying for his sick mare to get better and entrusting his ailing wife to the care of St Bridget.

When the opening hymn had ceased Father Mick, in his dark habit and white surplice, walked up and down the centre aisle calling out prayers which were repeated by the kneeling children, amongst whom both of the shawled women had little girls of their own. The two women's lips moved in prayer. Mother-like their eyes occasionally searched in the congregation for the children's heads. Admiring glances fell on them when discovered.

"Thank God they're wanted somewhere," the poor mothers thought, while their living yet critical glances travelled over the little heads to see if the coloured bows on their hair were still in order.

"Oul' Crumlin the Mill owner, chased my wee girls out of the mill yard and called them dirty brats" Mrs. Hanna whispered. With pride she looked towards where one of the 'dirty brats' was now praying. The child's clean little hands were joined and raised above a shining bright face in supplication.

"Because they don't be dressed as well as his childher they're not fit to be seen and there's no goodness in them to the like of Crumlin's breed."

"Let us say one Our Father, and three Hail Marys for your fathers, mother, brothers and sisters," called out the deep musical voice of Father Mick. To the united prayer of the children the church resounded, and the mothers joined earnestly. The rich might spurn their little ones but here at least they appeared to be welcome and a value, greater than gold, was placed upon their childish prayers.

"Yonders young Ned Brady," whispered Mrs. Hanna nudging her friend and signing the direction with her head.

Mrs. McCann looked to see the lad kneeling in attentive prayer near the altar. She little thought that, just at that moment, the hackler's son was almost in perspiration asking God to be near her daughter Sheila on her journey to America and beseeching him to allow them to meet again when his wages were big enough to keep them both.

"Now children behave yourselves" commanded the priest, unable to restrain a smile at discovering a fat little boy creeping below the seats to nip the bare legs of children near him. Getting the mischievous child back to his seat but still struggling with his smile his reverence continued to call out the prayers and lead the hymns until the service was over.

When the priest, who had said Mass left the altar the little ones were marshalled by their teachers and marched in order from the church. From the side chapels proud mothers and fathers lingering to say a few extra prayers watched them pass out while young men and young women hurried from the church to take up their accustomed positions outside the doors. On the broad walk above the steps little groups gathered here and there. Single young women formed a giggling group on one spot, single young men a circle on another.

When Ned Brady had left the building and reached the bottom of the steps he was confronted by Fissy Burns, a man of the mills. Fissy always fissed through a broken front tooth and was so nicknamed by the expression on Fissy's face it was evident he had something of interest to communicate. In an excited, but confidential way, he caught Ned by the arm and pulling him over to a quiet corner below the bushes asked, "Are ye going up to McBride's fields?" Scenting something starting, Ned replied by asking, "Why is there anything on?" Raising his brows Fissy emitted a "whoa," and with his eyes dancing in his head dramatically replied, "a slaughtering match, a slaughtering match. Arty Clarke and Jim Shanklin are settling oul' sores. It'll be murder, it'll be murder." This was indeed news to young Brady. He loved a fight and could not possibly resist the offer of such an exceptional attraction.

Everything was in it to ensure a tremendous battle. It had all the necessary ingredients, so to speak.

Both combatants were strong and young, both could stand punishment. They also lived in different Rows and worked in different mills. One was a rougher and the other a hackler, and most important of all they were of different religions. The young friends, therefore, lost no time in getting to the fields above the church.

Disputes of the week, if sufficiently serious, were always settled in McBride's field each Sunday morning. For some time past this particular fight had been brewing. It was to be a needle-contest, or as Fissy also said, was to let out a gathering of bad blood." Arty Clarke was the hackler, he worked in Ravage's Mill, while Jim Shanklin roughed in Ritchell's.

Naturally the workers took sides. There was trade rivalry, mill rivalry, street rivalry and religious rivalry and all these had to be settled by two men made murderous by the consciousness of them all. The news of the tussle had travelled. All the hacklers and roughers of the town appeared to have arrived in the district and taken up vantage points when the two friends reached the battle ground. A ring had been formed around which Fissy and Ned could hear remarks about the contestants. Clarke who was the younger of the two "had the stuff in him".

His father Billy Clarke the tenter had been a great fighter in the early days but when Billy's family grew up he left it behind and now looked upon fighting with disfavour. Indeed, he had become so bitter against it that everybody said he would not tolerate any of his family ever taking part in a fight at all. All the workers knew of this.

Around the grassy ring in which the two seconds stood grimly, the excited crowd surged eagerly watching for the men. Ned Brady looked around him. On the opposite side, to his surprise he detected his own father with a cap pulled far down over his eyes. Convenient to the elder Brady was his neighbour Bubbles Hanna, who had apparently hurried out of the church before the mass ended. The rougher's face was flushed his cough forgotten and from the point of his tongue tiny bright-bubbles flew above his head and floated away on the light breeze.

As young Brady glanced around, the fighters entered the circle of grass. Both were stripped to the waist and after a few remarks from the referee the fight started. Shanklin, a man of many battles and by far the burlier of the two looked indomitable. Clarke smaller, slimmer, and younger appeared a mere boy beside him. Shanklin's chest was black with hair, Clarke's white like a baby's. A few swings of the arms, a stagger by Clarke as if he had slipped, - crash, as Shanklin's powerful arm shot forward, a sickening noise like the sound of broken bones and the younger man collapsed in a heap with the blood gushing from his face. "Good God," ejaculated Fissy, "it's all over Ned." "My God what a dig," grunted someone in the rear. "That's the end of him," groaned another.

With both hands close to his bleeding face the injured fighter moved in pain upon the grass. A few feet distance, Shanklin, with his strong hands clinched in readiness and chest expanded stood with legs firmly planted on the ground and the killer-look upon his angry countenance. Young Brady watched him. Few expected Clarke to rise though many hoped he would. As the bleeding man tried to get up someone tried to raise a cheer. "He's up," said Fissy excitedly. Ned Brady looked just in time to see the wounded warrior shake his head like a terrier and rise from the blood-covered grass while Shanklin rushed in with a deluge of fierce swings to finish him.

Clarkes face and chest were completely covered with blood. In a dazed way he strove to ward off the attack, while keeping one of the hands to protect his face.

"Stop the fight. Stop the fight," several men yelled.

The sight of the staggering blood-covered young man was too much for them. He was unrecognisable. Others joined in the clamour.

"If he's a Clarke at all he'll not give in so easy," said an old man who had often seen Arty's father in action. Arty swayed and stumbled but in spite of Shanklin's hurricane attack was still on his feet. Everyone was breathless. Then a whisper passed from the edge of the ring. "The bridge of his nose is broken," it said, but the wounded man was still standing before his opponent.

At that moment Fissy Burns pulled Ned's sleeve. Nodding towards a small mound in the rear he directed him to look. To his astonishment Ned saw Arty Clarke's father just arriving at the back of the crowd. The old man began squinting and shading his eyes with his hand in an effort to recognise the fighters with his fading eyesight. Forty years of hard wear in the Mills had still left the broad frame but his work as a tenter had told its tale upon his eyes. Seeing the younger fighter covered in blood and not recognising his son old Clarke was heard to remark angrily, "It's a dammed shame, that lad's got enough." Young Clarke however was thinking differently. He was doing more now than just standing before Shanklin. Taking all that was coming to him he had already begun to bore in on his opponent. Step by step, with his face covered by one hand, he advanced. His other hand jerked out before him. After the first crash and the discovery that his nose had been broken no one thought he could possibly win with such a handicap. Spectators, therefore, speculated as to how long the lad would be able to hold out against the overpowering strength of his rival. Minute, however, succeeded minute and blow succeeded blow until by some miracle the blood-stained fighter appeared to become the stronger, with Shanklin showing signs of wear. Old Clarke, out of sympathy for the injured man and still not suspecting he was his own son had taken sides. His arms and body moved with the blows in the ring. He was carried away with excitement. Hacklers and roughers forgot their coughs. "Can Arty Clarke win?" was the question in everybody's mind. Shanklin's arm shot out, - crash, - many of the spectators closed their eyes and winced with Clarke as the blow fell upon the wounded fighter's nose. But the young man groaned, shook his head and continued pressing forward.

A bell rang. Somebody remarked, "There's the bell for twelve mass," but nobody showed any desire to hurry to prayers. A life and death struggle was going on before them. "He's a marvellous lad that," a voice said as thud, thud, the blows fell on Shanklin's face. The guarding hand deserted the wounded nose. It lashed out with the other. Old Clarke had forgotten his resolutions about fighting. "What a lad, what a heart," he was exclaiming as he danced excitedly on the mound behind Ned and Fissy.

A chorus of cheers rent the air. Someone shouted, "Keep quiet." The blood-stained fighter had flung himself upon his formidable opponent, crash, crash, a fierce shower of blows fell and with them Shanklin completely collapsed to be carried from the ring by his crest-fallen supporters.

The fight was over. Arty Clarke had won. Crowds surged towards the victor.

"There's yer da, Arty," one of the spectators said warningly to the hero. "Good God and I haven't been to mass yet," Arty answered, gathering up his clothes and hurrying out of the field. Across the road he ran with others in pursuit until he arrived in the club house where he dressed and holding a handkerchief to his nose hurried to the church.

Waving his stick above his head, old Billy Clarke had pushed forward to the ring shouting, "I've never seen such pluck. That's a great lad. I must shake his hand." But his son had been too quick for him, and by the time the old man had reached the ring, he was out of sight.

Disappointed, the father looked around in the hope of seeing someone he knew. Discovering Barney Bubbles, the rougher at a moment when Bubbles was trying to avoid meeting him.

"That was a great fight Barney," he began, "I didn't think

we had a lad in the town to stand up to Shanklin, tell me does he belong to here?" he asked.

Seeing that the old man had not recognised his son and knowing how bitter he had been against fighting Barney Bubbles avoided the question by merely remarking, "He's a grand lad."

But the excited tenter was not satisfied and asked loudly, "What do they call the boy?"

"Young Clarke," answered a man from a crowd of townspeople passing by. "Young Clarke, ye oul' fool" somebody else shouted. "Clarke, Clarke," repeated the old man. Then recalling the rougher's hesitation he stopped. Grabbing hold of his friend's shoulder he looked into his eyes and beseechingly pleaded. "My God, Barney, was it my boy Arty? Was it my poor boy Arty?"

Coughing sorely, the rougher timidly answered, "It was." Unable to say another word the astonished old man left his friend. Striking the ground with his stick and speaking to no one he thumped out of the field and down the big road.

On arriving at his home in the Row he found the table laid and tea and bacon prepared for his meal, but Old Clarke was too busy thinking to have much to say. As his wife put the bacon on the table he asked sharply, "Have ye no eggs?"

Surprised by his abrupt question the woman answered "I have only one and I am keeping it for yer breakfast in the morning. "Give it to Arty. Give it to the growing lad," he commanded. He needs an egg more than me," as he lapsed into silence and found his mind travelling back into his youth.

CHAPTER NINE

The Emigrant

The Monday following the fight in McBride's fields was the day of Sheila McCann's departure to America. That morning, Aunt Margaret, with the fine airs and gold ornaments had arrived early in the Row. The street was excited, and Sheila dragged off to the town in order to secure suitable clothing for the journey.

In the afternoon the shoppers returned laden with parcels. The wonderment of the inhabitants grew, and every time Aunt Margaret appeared a hundred eyes were gratified.

Mrs. McCann had "asked of her work" for the day and between trying to entertain her important visitor, attend to her own little children and get things ready for her girl's departure she was kept so busy she had no time to realise her daughter was leaving until bedtime had arrived that night.

At six o'clock the mills emptied themselves of their workers and batches of barefooted girls in shawls called to see the emigrant and bid her good-bye. Everyone, who could afford it and others who could not brought the girl a present. A farewell like this was worse than a death in the Row. At a death friends saw the end of the departed and a Christian burial was assured but no one could foretell what would become of Sheila McCann in a far-off foreign country.

Everybody, including the girl herself, were broken-hearted. Amidst all the excitement and preparations, the young girl thought of Ned Brady. Except for having seen the young man occasionally pass by the window she had not been able to be near him since the night they had walked up the steep white road to the dark hill and she dreaded having to say good-bye to him.

On his way home from work Barney Bubbles called. "Is Sheila in"? He asked between coughs, for Monday was always his worst day. At the sound of the familiar voice and cough the girl rushed to the door as the rougher pulled off his dirty cap and held down his head. A small parcel was slipped into the girl's hand as he asked with emotion, "Would it be asking ye too much to ask ye to bring this to my brother Dan. He lives near where yer going to in America and it's a wee bit of hackled flax and an old watch of our da's. Dan had his day at the hackling but he's now better off, and I'm sure he'd like to have the flax for oul' time's sake. Ye'll find the address on the cover an' I'd like ye to meet him and tell him we're all well," he explained.

"Certainly Barney," smiled Sheila taking the packet. She was thinking how she would miss seeing the familiar, humorous face and the sight of the tiny bubbles that he often blew at her as she passed.

Fumbling in his pockets, "I'll be down at the boat to see ye off," he continued extracting from his trousers a chunk of tobacco, a clay pipe, a knife, a pair of broken Rosary beads and some marbles. Fingering amongst the pile until he had discovered a bright half-sovereign, he handed the coin to the girl with a sigh of relief.

"That's from me and the wife," he said pushing it into her reluctant hand and rushing off before the girl had time to thank him.

Almost everyone in the Row appeared to have some friend in America, so the poor emigrant was laden with many parcels and messages. Aunt Margaret who had become hardened by the ways of the States didn't like this, but her niece understood and was pleased. While attending to the many callers at the door Sheila's eyes repeatedly searched the street for Ned Brady. Usually, the lad passed down before seven o'clock each evening but as that hour went by without any sign of his return, the young girl concluded that something serious must have happened. The time for her departure from the Row drew near, but although she ran a hundred times to the door, the young man did not come down the street.

Frequently glancing at the clock Sheila had begun to despair of seeing him before she left when a tall dark figure passed by the window. Without waiting for a knock, she rushed to the door and almost fell in the man's arms. It was Father Mick. The priest smiled as he entered the kitchen and shook hands with the widow and Aunt Margaret. Taking Sheila aside he gave her a medal and a rosary saying, "Here are a few souvenirs for you which I blessed specially for a safe journey." Then putting his hand in his pocket he drew out a sovereign which he gave her remarking pleasantly, "This is for luck," In subsequent years Sheila McCann would have told you that this coin and this luck had never left her.

"Oh, thanks, Father, it's too good of ye," was all she could say, but his reverence patted her shoulder and wishing an affectionate, "Good-bye and God bless you," left the house.

Through her tears she continued to watch the clock and the window. The time for departure was almost at hand, the visitors were leaving one by one, when a gentle knock was heard at the door. Everybody knew that knock. In the Row one was easily recognised by his or her knock.

"Its Mrs. Brady" remarked Mrs. McCann. Sheila's heart leaped as she opened the door.

Ned's shy mother was reluctant to enter but the persistence of Mrs. McCann and Aunt Margaret soon had her in the kitchen, where after looking round carefully, as if disappointed she asked, "Is our Ned not here?"

"Your Ned was never in this house in his life, except perhaps when he was a tiny child," Mrs. McCann, dreading that her gentle neighbour might think they had at any time harboured her boy.

"Why do ye ask?" modestly queried Sheila, seeing the look of disappointment on the woman's face.

The mother dropped her head as she replied, "It's strange, and it's not like him. He hasn't come home yet and Peter and me are very anxious about him", then by way of explaining her visit she looked at the young girl saying, "we thought, on account of Sheila going away tonight that he might have called in here on his way from his work."

The girl's heart fluttered. "He may have been kept late," suggested Mrs. McCann.

"God grant he's alright," replied the anxious woman. Kissing Sheila on the cheek and leaving a small parcel on the table without explanation she went out calling back, "I'll hurry down and let Peter know he's not here."

Ten minutes later Dan O'Neill's old side car bearing Aunt Margaret, Sheila McCann, her mother, and a neighbour-man to look after the luggage, set out from Ravage's Row. Blinds were drawn and tears fell as it drove along the street towards the broad road and turned the corner on its way to the docks. In the homes prayers were said and candles burned for the girl's safety. The crying screams of the McCann children were heard long after the car had passed out of sight.

At the boat old and young had gathered to give the emigrant a befitting send-off. Even Johnny Connor had left his cabin on the high mountain in order to wave farewell. In the centre of a group of noisy crying girls Sheila stood near the gangway. Beside the girls were gathered the older women who wept in silence beneath their dark shawls. Johnny Connor looked round for a pal and saw Barney Bubbles. "How's the cough," he asked when he pushed his way through the crowd. "As bad as ever" answered his friend coughing. Monday night was bad enough for a rougher without a sad affair like this, so Barney Bubbles coughed plenty. Sad things always made his cough worse. "I haven't seen ye up my way lately," remarked the man from the mountain. "It's getting too much for me nowadays," coughed the man from the mills. "Isn't it terrible about this poor wee girl going to

America," he asked as if wishing to avoid talking about himself. "All the young people want to be going. It's terrible," answered Johnny sharply. "All the best of our young people are going there. There's very little pickings here for hard work for them."

"That's true" said Barney Bubbles as the mountainy man angrily continued.

"The mills are grinding the souls out of the people and drops of tea and dip-bread are poor compensations for all that's expected from them and the young ones will be getting sick watching it." Barney Bubbles subdued a cough and nodded. An occasion like this always angered the hillman who went on talking. "They may get more tea in America but it's only escaping the kind of slavery for to enter another. No matter where they go, God help them, they'll carry the ghost of tomorrow's promised insecurity on their shoulders. It's a poor way for decent people to have to live in a world where there's so much of everything."

A stir near the two men made them look in its direction to see the hackler Peter Brady forcing his way towards them, Peter looked anxious. "Did any of ye see our Ned in the crowd?" he asked. Both men examined the gathering. "I don't think he's here, Peter. He's tall like yerself and easily noticed," said Johnny. "That's strange," mumbled the hackler turning to push his way to the other side of the crowd. A whistle sounded, a voice screamed, and everybody surged towards Sheila McCann who had already begun to say her good-byes. As the poor girl kissed them, each girl burst into tears and the older women covered up their faces with their shawls. "Thank

God it's not one of my children that's going," wailed a shawled figure to which another thankfully added, "nor mine."

The tears blinded Sheila. Passing from one to another she now and then glanced over the crowd in search of Ned Brady. But there was no sign of the young man. The boatmen had begun to call out, "Hurry up" "hurry up." When she reached the gangway where the last to grasp her hand was Peter Brady the hackler. By this time, she was unable to contain herself. Flinging her arms around the big man she broke into violent sobs. Tears trickled down the hackler's cheeks as affectionately he adjured her, "Cheer up girl. Ye'll be back again. Ye'll be back home again, with Gods help."

"Oh goodbye, Mister Brady. Goodbye, Mister Brady," the girl wailed and breaking away rushed up the gangway as the boat horn sounded. The girls and women wept, the men sniffed, Peter Brady was heartbroken for his son and the girl.

Reaching the side of her sedate Aunt Margaret the distracted emigrant strove to control her emotion. Both stood at the railings in full sight of the crowd. Aunt Margaret was waving and smiling, but her niece was straining through her tears in the hope of seeing young Ned Brady arrive at the quayside before the boat left.
When the boatmen had removed the gangway, one of the mill girls began to sing. This was a signal for the others. The farewell songs began: *'Come back to Erin Mavourneen, Mavourneen, come back aroon to the land of thy birth'*.

Aunt Margaret looked even more pleased. To her the singing was music in her honour. To the girl it was like a death knell. Standing dazed and staring far over heads of the assembled people she anxiously watched the entrance to the shed.

The song swelled over the waters, the boat chains rattled, and the voice of the captain bellowed out instructions. "Come back to Erin," sang the wailing waving crowd. "Would Ned never come?" rang in the girl's heart. "Would she never see him again?" she wondered. The boat was moving out. She began to pray. Suddenly someone came running through the far gate of the shed. Her heart bounded. It was Ned and he was hurrying. Oh, how she waved and waved and listened. The boat was gathering speed. The engines rattled. She strained to listen. Yes, above the singing and rattling she could hear his voice: "Come back to Erin," the crowd cried but amongst the melody Ned Brady's strong voice reached her.

"Good-bye Sheila," he was shouting. "Good-bye, Ned," she called. Her voice was weak. She strove to keep awake, her body swayed and collapsed in a faint as the melody continued and the young man remained calling and waving his handkerchief until the boat was far out on the Lough.

That night no one felt the parting more than the big hackler Peter Brady. The girl's burning broken-hearted kiss had melted him completely. When he had heard his son's voice above the din he was almost as pleased as the broken-hearted girl. "Where in the name of God were ye?" he asked tearfully, when the boat was out of sight and the waving has seized and he had been able to get near his boy. With lips that trembled, the lad sadly answered. "I had to work in, da, and I couldn't get away any earlier."

86

The father dried his eyes. He understood his son. It was no use talking about it, he thought, so thinking of Sheila McCann, father and son left the quay without any further conversation.

Johnny Connor accompanied by Barney Bubbles caught up with them on the way home. Hitting the young man on the back the mountain man whispered in the lad's ear. "The dark hill won't be the same now, Ned, it won't be the same."

CHAPTER TEN

Ned Brady's Job

Young Ned Brady's job in an office brought him in contact with a different class of people to what he had been accustomed.

"Actors," he thought, "actors," pretending to be bigger than they were and aping at being like rich people. They lived a precarious well-dressed existence and spurned the idea of being regarded as working people. Ned felt it difficult to fit in with the new class and often rebelled. In Ravage's Row the people admired the man who was a man but in this association they admired the fellow whose money enabled him to lord it over them, even though he were a cad. At home and at school the lad had always been addressed as Ned. In the office where he worked, he was called Brady.

"What is your father, Brady?" the son of his employer asked one day. To Ned his parents had always been Da, and Ma, but these people referred to their parents as Father and Mother. "A hackler," answered Ned.

An amused expression passed over the other's face and lingered long enough for the lad to notice it. "It must be beastly work," the boss's son remarked sneeringly, as he passed into his father's cosy office.

"What," wondered Ned, "would he think if he knew

my mother wore a shawl?" But despising the snob he continued his work. The boss himself was a man of much money and little patience. The money had come down to him from a line of business robbers and the impatience with it. Outside his factory he could not abide working people. Inside he only excused their existence in proportion to the profits they made him. God, he seemed to believe had created them especially for him. Not the delicate ones, of course, but the strong qualified ones.

Other than for making profits for him the only other job he would have given workers would have been fighting wars with other countries who dared to compete with him as an exporter.

In Ravage's Row to be generous hearted was the highest stamp of character. In the office it was a mug's game and had to be curbed if one were to keep his employment. To get on one was advised to be hard, mean, and crafty.

'Man mind thyself' was the boss's guiding gospel. To remind him, this motto, in large red letters, was always kept above his desk but he really did not require it. With the blood of workers, it was written all over him and all around his factory, the paler the workers cheeks, the redder the letters.

The business had been started by his father and the present owner had seen that parent, who was known as the *'slave-driver'* in action. The motto of *'keep the worker down to get the profits up'* had inspired both. If the poor slaves should ever rise, they feared they would want share. Slave-driving was, therefore, in the boss's blood. Nothing seemed to give him greater satisfaction than to see a hungry faced man bow before him and plead for a job. Like most mill-owners he found elevation in the doffing of caps and the beseeching's of workers. It gave him the feeling of great power.

Ned Brady's weekly wage was eighteen shillings and each Saturday this sum, was carried home unbroken to his mother. "That woman McMahon is no damned use," barked the boss one morning, "she's too old and too damned slow." The foreman to whom he had spoken required no further instructions. Old Bella McMahon who had given her best years to the tyrant's tyrant father and himself was sent home and she and her invalid sister could go to hell as far as the boss was concerned.

Such happenings while stunning Ned Brady made him prouder of and more loyal to his own class. He knew the painful dreads that forever haunted the minds of the working people. The boss and his class seemed far removed from them.

Profits had to be made at all costs. The owners steeled themselves to the machines and on went the scheme making it harder and harder for good people to retain their virtue and easier for brutal scoundrels to flourish.

Would he eventually have to surrender to the boss's conception of life or always be able to retain his own? This was a question that confronted the young man. To a less manly lad the retaining of the good qualities given him in Ravage's Row would have been no easy task, but Ned Brady loved his own class with a loyal love, and though he saw and heard much that astonished him in his new world he kept his counsel and preserved with his work. To prevent his mind from being continually pained by thoughts of his separation from Sheila McCann he worked hard, but he was unable to drown the sound of the girl's hysterical *'Good-bye, Ned'*. In his ears it rang often and with it the birds and heather of the big dark hill came rushing into his head in spite of all his application. During one of these flashes the boss opened his office door and bawled "Brady." Ned jumped from his stool. It was a rude awakening, but he hurried to the private 'sanctum'.

Reaching a letter, the boss said, "I want you to take this letter to my house and bring me back an answer and go quickly."

Thinking he detected anger in the voice, he took the letter and donning his cap left the office.

A beautiful broad drive through a huge garden led to the owner's residence which was situated in the aristocratic quarter of the town. The young man walked along the drive and reached the entrance. At the door a frightened looking servant told him to wait. With cap and letter in hand he stood on the elevated step admiring the flowers around him.

"Won't you come inside?" a girl's voice asked. The young man turned to be confronted by a vivacious, vividly attired young girl of about his own age. Following her he was led into a large room that bewildered him. In his home in Ravage's Row the kitchen was parlour, dining-room, drawing-room, sitting room and smokeroom. Where he found himself was a sumptuous apartment, and he did not know what heading to put it under. So many articles of furniture and such variety of colour met him that he was dazed. Before he had time to collect his thoughts the girl had taken the letter from his hand saying very politely, (Ned thought too politely). "Won't you sit down; you'll have to wait. The letter's for mother and she'll be here at any moment."

Ned sank in a soft chair and tried to look comfortable. The girl continued talking. Gradually his eyes left the furniture and began to take stock of the girl. Without asking he knew she was the boss's only daughter. There was something about the eyes that told him that. As he examined her appearance she talked about the weather. Her teeth and lips were perfect. Now and then she moved restlessly on the thick coloured carpet. What a lovely young body she had, it seemed overcharged with life.

Something she said made her laugh and she tossed her head. Such a wealth of glorious tresses responded to the movement and what bewitching colour surrounded her open smile. Whatever kind of light red material her dress was made off, it tried to hide and expose her curved body at the same time. "Are you long with my father?" she asked, coyly drawing nearer to where Ned sat.

"Over two years," the lad answered, shyly looking towards the door and hoping for the early arrival of the mother. "What college were you at?" she questioned, touching the edge of the young man's chair with her knee. Recalling the expression on her brother's face when he had told him his father was a hackler he gruffly answered, "I was never at a college."

To his surprise the girl laughed. "You didn't miss much. I have been at one for three years and have refused to go back. Father wants me to remain, but I want to go to business so there's a row on and the home's a bit of hell at present."

Swinging her arms and swaying as if dancing she winked cutely as she sang rather than said, "I'll have more freedom, college is a bore, I mean to have more freedom."

The door opened noiselessly, and an elderly woman entered. "Oh, here's mother now" exclaimed the girl running to reach the woman the letter. Taking the communication to the window where she opened it the boss's wife read it twice. Then sitting down at the edge of a large table she wrote a reply which was carefully put in an envelope and handed to the young man. Between the mother and daughter there appeared to be a coldness. Even the size of the room seemed to accentuate it. Much relieved, the lad, with a hurried bow, took his departure for the office where on arrival he found the boss walking up and down in a temper.

When the young man entered, he darted to meet him. Snatching the letter from his hand he opened and read it.

"I'll teach her, I'll teach her," he repeated. Then stamping towards Ned's desk, with eyes blazing in his head, he viciously instructed, "Brady, my daughter will start in this office tomorrow morning. She'll help you and I want her to get plenty of work. Start her at making out the new ledgers, give her plenty to do damn her," repeating the "damn her" he grunted and breathlessly rushed into his private office, slamming the door after him.

CHAPTER ELEVEN

Sylvia Bennington

About an hour after all the members of staff had arrived at her father's office, Sylvia Bennington sailed in next morning. "The spy has come," one whispered while another wrote, "dressed for a ball," on a bit of paper and threw it to a friend. With one eye on his work, Ned Brady had watched for her arrival with the other, and made preparations for her occupation. New books littered the desk.

"Good morning, Mister Brady," Sylvia saluted when, after hanging up her coat and hat and adjusting her hair, she at last reached his desk. Nobody had ever called him Mr Brady before and Ned did not know whether to like it or not. At home he was just plain Ned. In the office he was just Brady, so the "Mister" shocked him a little particularly as it came from the boss's daughter.

"I am to commence here today, and father told me you would be kind enough to show me what to do," the girl said pleasantly taking up a position beside him. Ned nodded. In a few moments he had started to show her what she had to do. He wanted to waste no time. "You are to transfer all the names from the oul' ledgers into these new ones," he explained immediately, proceeding to outline exactly how this was to be done.

The desk was a high one. As he talked Miss Bennington flung herself into a high stool, crossed her legs and began playing pit pat with a pen on her beautiful teeth. "How long will it take me to do that?" she asked wearily as soon as her instructor had finished explaining. "Ten or twelve days," replied the young man half expecting her to leap down and make off.

With an examining glance that ran over Ned's hair, face and form the girl dipped her pen the in the ink-well and with a "very well, here goes," began the work.

Leaving her with the books her instructor went to the far end of the long desk where he settled at his own job, but it was not long until he heard the polite voice calling, "Mister Brady" again. Stepping down from his seat he went to her assistance.

"How is this to be entered?" she asked. Giving her the necessary information, he resumed his seat only to be aroused by the call of "Mister Brady" more than fifty times until he became sick if the "Mister" and sick of the girl.

All that day the boss never appeared in the office, so that having being monopolised by the daughter young Brady was glad when closing time arrived. Miss Bennington, however, had been thinking. She was determined to accompany him part of the way home and when he left the office she was by his side and enquiring sweetly, "What way do you go home, Mister Brady?"

Reluctantly he answered, "Up the Crumlin Road."

"Oh, that's lovely," she delightedly exclaimed, "We'll be part of the way together."

To the young man's annoyance Sylvia trotted down the stairs and along the street beside him.

"Do you live far up the Crumlin?" she asked, prancing on his left. "Yes, away up at the top," Ned slowly explained. Noticing some of the office staff watching from the other side of the street, he was angry.

"Do you walk all the way? The girl persisted, looking over his strong young figure. "Yes, I always walk it," he answered. "Do you walk to your work in the morning?" she asked. "I do," came the sharp reply.

With his long strides Ned was making it necessary for his companion to trot. What would the workers say, what would the boss think? And what would be the remarks of the neighbours in the Row if they saw him with the girl Bennington? What would Sheila McCann think? Striding on he asked himself these questions. "You walk very fast, Mister Brady," remarked the voice at his side, Ned shortened his stride. He would have liked to run instead, but continuing their walk, Miss Bennington strove to be as pleasant and tempting as possible. Glancing now and then at the far away summit of the big dark hill which was now visible and thinking of the girl who had left for America, the young man walked and listened until he found relief when at last they parted at the corner of the Antrim Road, and he was left to continue the remainder of the journey alone.

All that week Sylvia's "Mister Brady" and her small talk were showered upon her instructor. Sparing no effort, she endeavoured to impress him but as Barney Bubbles would have said, "The butter came through the brochan." She was too gushing in her attention. Each evening, however, although the young man tried to avoid her, she managed after leaving the office to walk part of the way in his company.

On one of these walks they travelled via Clifton Street when two women from the mills passed by. "Look at the shawlies," gurgled Sylvia, "Aren't they horribly dirty? Her voice was polished but Ned, as he thought of his own mother and her shawl winced. Then picturing the gushing girl's brother and grim father he tightened his lips and walked on without replying.

"There are plenty of shawlies and bare feet people up your way Mister Brady," she went on, "Father says they wouldn't be happy any other way. They're like pigs, they love the gutter."

Making no reply, the lad stemmed his indignation as he pictured himself the kindly people of Ravage's Row and found himself contrasting them with the Bennington's to the latter's disadvantage. To him, Sylvia's dress, no longer looked pretty. She had become another whip that fell upon the shoulders of himself and his kind. The ruined bodies of his class had provided everything to build and beautify hers and she would vomit on them.

The pain of her remarks tortured him. He hated her thoughts. Arriving at their parting place near the Antrim Road they were about to separate when he saw Barney Bubbles and his wife approach. Bubbles had just left the roughing-shop. He wore his old torn clothes and was covered with tow and pouce. His hair was sticking out from tears in his cap. Mrs. Hanna had a torn shawl over her shoulders. They looked mill-worn. The rougher and his wife were almost abreast the young couple before they recognised them. Suddenly Bubbles saw Ned and whispered to his wife, "There's Ned Brady."

The poor woman immediately lifted her shawl from her shoulders and drew it well over her head and face. "That's a swell girl he has with him," whispered the rougher pulling his cap down to his nose and turning his head in the opposite direction to the young pair.

Thinking Ned Brady had not recognised them they were just passing when they heard the lad's melodious voice ring out with more than its usual friendliness.

"Hello Mrs. Hanna, hello Barney," Mrs. Hanna did not look but her husband glanced towards his young friend in time to see him raise his cap with great gusto.

"Another young man in Ned's position wouldn't have wanted to notice us, and us in our working clothes and him with such a swell," the rougher remarked when he was out of hearing. His wife nodded in agreement. Rather proudly she pushed her shawl back upon her shoulders and fixed her hair. At the thought of Ned Brady, in spite of his company, not disowning his friends both were made happy.

"Do ye know who the young lady is?" Mrs. Hanna asked when far down Clifton Street. "I heard them say it's that oul' skinflint Bennington's daughter," replied Bubbles. "Merciful God," exclaimed the woman, "It's bad enough to have to work for the likes of them but I'll swear their company's neither good for man nor beast."

Bubbles coughed and blew out a string of Bubbles. "Stop that nasty habit," said the wife sharply. Her husband continued. "They're a bad lot I believe but although nobody else has a good word to say about them, I never heard Ned Brady say anything to their detriment yet and it appears he's with that girl often."

The woman tugged at her shawl as she muttered, "I'll warrant ye the poor lad earns every farthing they give him, but he's far too good for the likes of that hussy or any of her breed."

Talking in this strain the Hanna's pursued their journey. That night Ned Brady reached home feeling proud that Miss Bennington's disparaging remarks about shawlies had stung him into proclaiming his allegiance to his class. No longer could her presence in the office be even interesting, in fact it became an increasing torture.

So much was the young man irritated by her talk and approaches that, on the following Saturday afternoon, he went up to the mountain heather in order to take stock of his position with the Bennington's. On the top of the dark hill he could think without distraction.

Johnny Connor had said it would not be the same without Sheila McCann and Johnny was right. Every tree, every bird, every flower, spoke of her absence. The mountain man himself very forcibly reminded him of her as soon as he had reached the cabin at the top of the steep white road.

Standing outside the door with a large stick in his hand, Johnny's greeting was, "No word from the wee girl yet Ned?" To which the lad replied, "It's too soon! Johnny. It's too soon to have any word."

"Mrs. McCann's keeping well considering the loss of her girl so soon after the death of her man," remarked the

Hillman. Ned did not want to talk. His mind was too full. He wished to be alone with the mountain. The parting with Sheila, the annoyance of Sylvia Bennington, the discomfort of his present position. These were the things he wanted to ponder over, and he craved to be by himself in the heather above the cabin, but Johnny wanted to talk.

"I see they're building another mill down there on the side of the Crumlin Road," he said pointing towards the town with his stick. The young man nodded. "Another jail for making more pale faces and blood profits twelve hours every day," snarled the farmer.

Ned looked at the face of the speaker. It was flushed and angry as its eyes glared down at the big mills.

"They'll make a grand comfortable place to suit their machines," he sneered, "And build more pigsties for the human beings that work them. The machines'll be well oiled and happed up, but the workers will go on their bare feet and continue to starve," waving his stick at the town the big man turned to Ned as he added gloomily, "There's no thought for the people, there's no thought at all for the poor people, damn it, the people'll have to think for themselves."

Becoming interested by Johnny's warmth the lad asked quietly, "Will the increasing mills not improve their lot Johnny?" "Nonsense," bellowed his friend, "As long as they slave for little, they'll get little and when they ask for more, more slaves and more subservient whites in some other part of the world will get the work and they'll be idle, that's the way it goes. Profits are all that's wanted and if they don't arrive the mills close down here and open where there's greater mugs to exploit."

"But some get on," smiled Ned.

"Aye" said the Hillman bitterly. "A few get fat at the expense of the many but the many get plenty of poverty. Everybody sings about the few who become successful exploiters, but nobody weeps for the many who're exploited and who never get anything or anywhere."

"And do ye really think Johnny, the mills wont eventually do good?" asked Ned.

"They couldn't do good," snapped the hillman, "They're not run for doing good for the people. They're bound to make the workers do any surrendering and sacrificing that's got to be done. Good people have come to them from all parts of the country and they are made bitter. I know them and they are all of grand oul' stock, dying to be good but finding it more difficult every day."

Ned agreed. He knew the workers of the mill rows. He knew how they strove to be generous to each other on a few shillings weekly, and how they paid for it. He knew how the parents loved their children and were daily tortured by not being able to buy them boots, clothes, and nourishing food. He knew how many of them strove to cure themselves without a doctor with dire results, rather than leave their little ones short of milk and bread. He knew of their continual struggle to retain all the virtues that the old clan culture of the surrounding country had given them in their childhood.

He was not too young to be able to see in this effort to pass through life in the rising industrial town the battle to keep what was left of a communal way of living.

"You are right Johnny," he said, "they are grand people and

it's heart-rending to watch them being tortured."

The hillman walked towards the door, where, with a wave of his stick he signed towards the heather and apologetically explained, "I've a job waiting me in the house, so I'll be going then," with a broad smile he added looking up at the heather, "Take another step up to dreamland, get up nearer the sky!"

Turning over in his mind the remarks of his friend, young Brady left the yard and climbed up to the heather above the cabin where he sat down.

The spot he had selected was just a few yards from the place where the girl Sheila and himself had lingered on the previous Sunday. Like a magnet it drew him towards it so he got up and was soon occupying the same spot from which he had talked to the girl so much. His had passed gently over the grasses she had rested on as his mind wandered back to their conversation. In thoughts of her there was no room for Miss Sylvia Bennington except when he felt angry that such a girl as Sylvia could remain at home and have plenty whereas Sheila had to go away to America.

After a while his eyes fell on the town over which the week's smoke appeared to lie heavily. As he tried to see through the clouds, he began to take stock of his young life and strove to glance into the future. "What," he wondered, "Would it hold for him and, what for Sheila?" His plans, since he had been able to make plans at all had always included his mother and father. Now Sheila was also in them. These three were to be the occupants of his castles.

For over two years he has worked in Bennington's progress had been slow, but he was patient and easily satisfied. The coming of Miss Bennington, however, had upset his patience. No money could compensate him for having to be scourged continually by contact with her. In the quietness of the mountain he decided he would watch the papers and apply for another job. A change of position would help to relieve his mind of some of the painful thoughts his separation from his girl had brought. Sheila had promised to write to him as soon as she arrived in America. He was looking forward to receiving her letter. As he sat there counting the days and fingering the grasses a footstep on the hill above aroused him. Looking up he saw the valiant young fighter of the previous Sunday.

"Great Scot is it you Ned?" asked Arty Clarke as Ned got up from the heather and joined his young friend on the walk back down the big hill. "How's yer nose?" asked Ned looking at the still swollen and discoloured organ. Making little of his injury the fighter smilingly remarked, "Oh it's alright," and they walked on. "It was a great fight and a greater victory," said Ned. Arty laughed. Putting his hand to his nose he commenced rubbing it affectionately as he remarked. "If Shanklin hadn't given me this at the start I don't believe I would have beaten him. The nose angered me terribly and I just had to beat him to save it."

Proceeding briskly along the steep white road the two young men continued their conversation until they at last parted near Ravage's Row. When they had separated Arty dryly called to his friend, "Yer on a winner now Ned, the Bennington's have plenty of money," just as a shawled woman whom Ned Brady knew was the widow McCann passed by.

CHAPTER TWELVE

Johnny Connor's Horse

P rayers and other attentions did not keep the life in Johnny Connor's mare. It died after a short illness and its owner wept. The man of the mountain had had Jinny for over ten years. He knew her and she knew him. As Peter Brady said, "They were a fine team," and Johnny understood every turn in the animal.

Jinny was likeable and obedient. She came when she was called, stopped when told to, and a baby could play with her without risk. When she died Johnny lost a friend. But the new horse, Rory, the Hillman bought to take her place, was an entirely different proposition. The rattle of the tin could not coax him from the heather. He wandered far and scampered into places he should not have visited, thus getting his owner into bother. He had a temper, was independent and objected to instructions.

"That rascal of a horse has a mind of his own. Jinny was a first-class servant, but this fellow hasn't the slave mind and it's going to be a job giving him one. He wants to go his own way all the time and ye can't blame him, but that doesn't suit me."

Thus, Johnny Connor addressed Peter Brady who had come up to the hill to sympathise with him on the loss of his mare. "Jinny was a pal in affliction, Peter. Manys a comforting hour she gave me," continued the hillman sadly. "When we were out with the milk together and it's raining, manys a cheering glance she had for me and us drenched, as if she meant to say, 'Carry on, Johnny, this is our lot'."

Peter thought he saw a tear fall on the strong man's vest, "She's a great loss to ye and it will be hard to fill her place," the hackler said consolingly.

"Hard!" replied Johnny as he looked towards the hilltop. "It would be impossible, why when I was sick, I've seen that mare come down from the heather a dozen times in the day and push its head in over the half-door to see if I was better, the poor thing, ye would have thought it was asking how I was."

"She was very wise," remarked his friend, watching the hillman's emotion.

"Wise, man she was wise," replied Johnny. "It's only me that knew the wisdom of Jinny, and to think the poor thing struggled on in sickness and never lost her patience is heart-breaking. Just like many of the self-sacrificing human beings made martyrs in the crazy way of living of today."

"The new horse may turn out alright, Johnny, when ye get him into yer own way," said his friend hopefully.

"Get him into my own way," sneering Johnny, gazing up at the summit. "That devil. I'll never be able to do a thing with him. Sowl he's well named Rory. He's as wild as the hill. Yesterday, with his antics he spilled a can of milk and left me short for many of my customers. They say the man's a slave to the machine and the horse a slave of man, but this gentleman's going to make me his slave, by the look of things." The hackler smiled. "He must be a bothersome fellow."

"Bothersome," snapped Johnny, "I have to get up an hour earlier every morning to get him yoked and if he ever gets up on the heather all the calling in the world wouldn't get him down again. Even when he's out in the cart it's not every door he'll stop at. If he doesn't like the place, he's halted at he prances. If he doesn't like a person, he snaps at them and all along the way he tries to hurry me with the result I'm not worth tuppence when I get home each day."

"Just like oul Billy Clarke the tenter," interjected Peter, "Snappy and restless."

"Now yer talking," shot Johnny promptly. "Horses are just like human beings; some make good slaves and some don't. Jinny had the breed of slaves in her bones, but Rory wants his own way. If I pull the reins at all he shakes his head and gets into a fit of temper. I let them loose he just goes wherever he's in the humour to go. Even when we've finished our rounds he doesn't want to come home at all whereas Jinny got her greatest happiness coming back home. Do ye know I think this fellow objects to me living on the top of a hill."

Beckoning, to his friend to follow, the Hillman moved into the house. Inside the two men sat down by the fire. Peter on the side near the wee window which the hill's slope almost touched, and Johnny in his favourite seat beside the door.

"Ye're very welcome Peter," said Mrs. Connor continuing

her flowering of handkerchiefs near the table.

"Thank ye, it's a nice day, Mrs. Connor," said Peter. The hillman's wife was a quiet-spoken industrious wee woman, who had the poorest of health. She never talked much but when asked why, always answered, "Johnny can do the talking for both of us."

Once seated by the fire the hillman took down his pipe and was soon puffing. Peter Brady didn't smoke but found pleasure watching the movements of his friend's jaws and his wife's fingers.

"That's a fine lad of yours," began Johnny when his pipe was going to his satisfactions. His friend smiled at the reference to his son.

"Oh, yes, he's a good lad and I hope and pray he does well," he remarked. The hillman was thoughtful as he puffed, then bending over towards his friend, he said knowingly, "He'll see big changes if he's spared."

"We've seen a lot of changes ourselves," drawled the hackler, at which the flowering woman nodded, sadly.

Johnny grew restless with his thoughts. Hitting the bowl of the pipe sharply on the heel of his boot he grunted, "Plenty of changes, plenty of changes for the few but little for the many. The poor are still as poor as I ever remember them, but the rich are getting richer and the richer they get the poorer the poor become."

"But there's more work now," said Peter, questionly.

Johnny put his pipe on the fireplace and replied heatedly. "Plenty of work, sowl there's plenty of work in yer town but little else and they call it by the sacred name of work but what is given for it! Why my mare Jinny had a better living and this horse Rory although he doesn't deserve it will be better treated. What would you call being forced to bring up a family on a pound a week? Its only slavery, it's only wage slavery."

The hackler rubbed his head, "No one knows the people's struggle better than I do and I agree it's terrible. Their machines and their animals get far better care than we do."

The name of machines always annoyed Johnny. "Machines, machines," he growled, "When there's anything the matter with one of them the bosses always rush to attend to it but none of them are ever seen hurrying to attend a hacklers or roughers or spinner's funeral.

The hillman got up from his chair and began stamping up and down the earthen floor. Over her needlework Mrs. Connor smiled knowingly. Realising that the Mill affairs always roused his friend, Peter Brady endeavoured to change the subject. A gentler theme was needed so the hackler thought of fairies.

"Tell us," he asked, "do the folk around the hill here ever talk of fairies?" The stamping ceased and the hillman, in thoughtful humour again lifted his pipe from the fireplace, lighting it he resumed his chair, as his friend continued, "In the part of the country where I come from there are still many people who believe in them, and my son Ned never wearies of hearing about the wee folk."

Johnny drew his chair back from the fire. Adopting a voice

suitable to the subject he answered softly, "Fairies, fairies, why my mother and father, God rest them, would have sworn they had seen fairies." "And so would mine," added Peter.

Johnny was pensive, he seemed to be regretting the change of subject, "God knows I used to believe in them myself but now I don't, and I suppose yer the same. It's wonderful how we leave the oul' notions behind us as we grow oulder and take on new ones."

"True enough for you Johnny but I still like to hear of the wee people," remarked Peter.

His friend hit his pipe against his boot. "My own opinion about fairies," he began sharply, "it's that the tortured poor people of bygone years must have created them. The masters in those days who had power over them were unmerciful and the slaved crathers tried to imagine some people, some friends, with power on their side. They created the fairies and made them tiny so that they might be all the more able to escape the sight of the grinding masters and ye notice they made them always help the poor and afflicted."

"It's a strange explanation," remarked the townsman, "but do ye not think they had some connection with a great ancient race of people that used to live in Ireland in bygone ages."

Jumping to his feet Johnny flung his pipe on the fireplace. "Ancient race, be-damned," he shouted as he again began stamping up and down the floor. "Great races don't need relief," he bawled. "Poor people do, and the poorer they are the more they welcome fairies. Property, power, stocks, and shares are what the rich go in for. They haven't much time for ghosts or fairies. Damn them, the fairies never went to them."

As Johnny stamped, Peter laughed, and Mrs. Connor quietly remarked. "That man of mine can even lose his temper when he's talking about fairies."

The excited Hillman grunted. Shaking his head, he again lifted his pipe and resumed his seat.

"It always angers me," he explained, "when I think of what our fathers and mothers had to come through and what good people have still to endure in this way of living that's on them at present and will be until the world gets wiser."

"I get angry betimes myself, when I see how goodness is being destroyed," agreed Peter.

"Destroyed is the word, Peter," said Johnny, "but the pity of it all is that the poor people are so patient and so long-suffering like my late Jinny. Instead of flying into a rage about things that concern their bodies they fly to God and ask him to do jobs they should be doing themselves."

Peter bowed, "Gods their only consolation," he murmured.

Mrs. Connor still at her flowering, quietly interrupted. "I think I hear footsteps of someone coming down the hill pad."

All three sat listening. The footsteps drew nearer. In the yard they echoed as they passed the cabin. The head and shoulders of their owner moved by the half-door on his way to the town.

Peter Brady recognised the face. It was that of Barney Bubbles the rougher, who at that moment was launching a sparkling bubble from his tongue.

"That'll be company for me down the hill," the hackler said, jumping from his seat and searching for his cap.

Shaking hands with his two friends, who unsuccessfully tried to persuade him to remain longer, he left the cabin to catch up on his fellow-worker.

Entering the yard, he was astonished to discover that the coughing rougher was almost a hundred yards away and striding on with an unusually vigorous step. With the sitting, Peter's legs had stiffened so that he was walking some time before they had relaxed properly. He wouldn't call after his friend but decided to give him the 100 yards start and catch up with him on the way. This was how Peter reasoned, as in pursuit of the rougher, he strode along the path towards the steep white lane. After five minutes speedy walking, however the athletic hackler had not gained a yard. Always delighting in his prowess as a walker Peter Brady increased his pace. It would give him great joy to catch up and pass his friend who had now turned into the steep white road and was travelling splendidly. With long strides both men walked but after another five minutes Peter Brady had not reduced the hundred yards start by more than twenty. This was a surprise to the strong hackler who as he walked recalled the frail condition of his opponent, a few Sundays previously.

When half of the journey was covered Peter stretched

his stride to its fullest and the race went on with the rougher still holding the lead and the hackler gaining slowly. Passing people paused to smile at the racing pair but noticing no one Barney Bubbles with his eyes fixed on the road before him swung by. In the excitement he had forgotten his cough while the ears of the pursuing hackler were continually alert in the hope of hearing it. With Peter slowly but steadily gaining the two men reached the bend of the road that led to Ravage's Row. On down the broad way they walked while passers-by laughed at their perspiring faces and gazed after them admiringly. On entering the Row Barney Bubbles had lost most of his lead but was still some eight yards ahead of his friend. To wipe this out Peter Brady made a final burst in the hope of passing the rougher before he reached his own door. But his opponent also made a last spurt and in the race down the Row succeeded in reaching the door of his own house in time to stand in the hall and tantalisingly smile back, "Hello Peter," as his heated pursuer flew by.

Opening the kitchen door, the rougher entered the house where he collapsed in a chair and between coughs called upon his wife to bring him whiskey quickly.

In the Brady's home it dawned upon the hackler how he was "had" by his friend and more cold water than usual was thrown about his steaming face as he growled to his wife, "A nice laugh they'll have at me in the hackling shop tomorrow; that fellow's cough's only a confounded invention."

CHAPTER THIRTEEN

The Dark Hill

I n contrast to the hatred Johnny Connor of the Dark Hill had for the growing town, the workers of the mills loved the big broad mountain where Johnny lived. To them it was a magnet, the attraction of which few could resist. To young Ned Brady it was a huge idol commanding his continual worship. Wandering home from his work each evening his eyes, after their long starvation of scanning ledgers, feasted on it. As he walked he tried to imagine his feet sinking in its thick heather.

To locate Johnny Connor's small white cabin resting on its far-away sky-touching brow was a delight, and when the lad's eyes had discovered the house, they then sought to locate the spot where Sheila McCann and he had sat. For him a new life seemed to have begun there. In that big dark hill there was company that only a towny could understand. Ned's father often said he "couldn't live without it." Each Sunday the older Brady travelled its slopes but each day his eyes wandered up to where his feet had been. During the working week hungry eyes of busy workers often peered through the dim dirty mill windows to get a glimpse of the massive dark green whale, and they would have told you that it did them good. Deprived of almost everything else the poor people had at least their sight, and the beautiful picture of the majestic hill was everybody's property.

Fortunately, it was not an easy task to starve their eyes, and if such a thing had been done it would have made them less efficient slaves, so they were spared their eyesight.

Young and old loved the dark hill. Children in mill rows longed for the day when they could go gathering flowers and bird-nesting upon its slopes. The old nursed and cherished the remembrance of the happy hours when their once supple legs had enabled them to climb to its heather. By its presence the parents were daily reminded of their sweet hearting days.

The mountain soil above Johnny Connor's had also been wet by many a tear. To it the worker who had got the sack and was terrorized by thoughts for his family often wandered to weep and think, while the man who had a sick child or had lost a member of his household could cry and pray up there. Throughout the year the hillman had secretly watched many strong workers sob like babies on the dark heather.

Resolutions were also made up there. It was on the think heather young Ned Brady had resolved to get a new job. In those days that was not difficult for a young man of his type and as old Bennington always appeared to enjoy parting with his workers better than increasing their wages, Ned was to be relieved at the end of the following week, and it was arranged he should work late each night so that Miss Sylvia would have an opportunity of learning all about the work she had to take over on his departure.

"Give her a good drilling before you go," was the

instruction of his boss so Ned decided to work in each night until nine o'clock. After six o'clock all the other office hands went home, and the young man and the boss's daughter were left to themselves.

Miss Sylvia was most attentive. In fact, she was too attentive.

On the Friday night, which was to be the last of the overtime, the young girl for the first time remarked, "I am very sorry you are leaving Mister Brady." They were both sitting on high stools at a high desk as she spoke.

Ned by this time was thoroughly sick of her "Mister Brady," and continued his work without replying. There was still much entering to finish so he wanted no talk. The girl left her stool and standing near him said feelingly, "You'll be terribly missed by my father, Mister Brady." As he thought of old Bennington, he smiled to himself but remained silent as the girl called out the figures for him to make the entries in another book.

"I'm sure a smart young man like you would have got on well with my father," she remarked moving closer to Ned's stool. The young man looked at the clock. It was past nine and he wrote quickly. The office was warm. Receiving no reply, the girl continued calling out the figures. Her warm bare arm moved closer and closer towards the young man's shoulder and her soft plump young breasts crushed themselves painfully against the hard desk. Ned's mind was on his work. To finish with old Bennington, to begin in his new position were his inspirations.

"You'll call in and see us now and then and tell us

how you are getting on Mister Brady," crooned the soft voice at his shoulder. Ned smiled and continued writing. Sylvia pressed her bare arm against his coat and kept it there, her eyes drank in the grace and strength of her instructor's neck and shoulders.

Used to pampered young men who said flattering things and pawed she was thinking Mr Brady was different and therefore more attractive. Her arm pressed closer.

"Are you sure that balance is £21 – 6 – 7?" asked Ned sharply.

"Oh, I'm very sorry, I'm very sorry, it's my mistake, it should have been £27 – 16 – 1," the flushed girl explained apologetically. Ned solemnly corrected the figures.

"You'll require to be very careful in posting, Miss Bennington," he remarked without raising his head.

The girl turned over to the next page and after reading an entry removed her breasts from the hard desk.

The hands of the clock had travelled round and only a few more pages remained to be called out.

"You won't forget to come and see us Mister Brady," said the girl almost pleadingly. Ned nodded. As he did so the hot white breasts now marked by the hard wood of the desk were pressed against his side while the warm arm moved down gently on his coat. When the entries were finished the young man began to look back over his work and Sylvia leaned over his shoulder.

Already she could feel the pain caused by the hard wood leaving her breasts as she strove to spread them against the young man's side.

"It must be a relief to you to have that job done," she murmured softly and enquiringly.

Ned bowed and turned over the pages. Sylvia felt the warmth of the strong young form beside her and slowly pressed closer. As her instructor paused at a page she pushed her flushed face over his shoulder and strove to bend her figure around him. Gradually a shapely foot found rest on the rung of his stool and a warm thigh moved gently upwards towards his leg. The pages were turned over quickly, then another pause and the girl pressed her breasts forward and the thigh upward until the heats of both young bodies seemed like one. Ned touched his brow and went on with his work.

"Is that one correct?" she asked now and then. Ned paused and she pressed.

Having begun her advance very gently, with each pause her pressure had increased until now her fingers had gripped the cloth of the young man's coat below his right arm.

The work was almost completed when he became conscious of the increasing warmth against him. The girl had become more daring. Her sparely clad young body strove to penetrate the rough tweed of the busy clerk, her hot breath burned his neck, her fingers tightened on his coat, her left foot sought his, her waist curved in a mad effort to force her body more tightly against him, the last page of the ledger was reached. Ned shivered and shaking his back like an irritated lion picked up the book, bounded from his stool and hurried to the safe.

Crest fallen the aroused girl flung her arms on the desk and the lad thought he detected a tone of viciousness in the voice that forgetting the "mister" said, "You're too blasted cold Brady."

Coming back to the desk and picking up the other books he placed them carefully in the safe while Sylvia, with flushed face, and sinking breasts stood silently fighting with herself. The young man's mind had flashed to America. A pardonable pride had taken possession of him. At that moment the memory of poor Sheila McCann was more welcome to him than all the advances of rich Sylvia Bennington.

His work for the day completed, he felt he could not get home quickly enough so after closing the office he and the girl walked speedily towards the Junction. Miss Bennington assumed an air of offended dignity whilst he discovered a new strength. On the way there was little talk. Their kind, thought Ned, "only play with ours." Often, he had heard the men of the mills say that and he believed that Sylvia only wanted to play with him. As they walked, he congratulated himself on having been wise to her approaches. Seeing a Crumlin Road tram at the junction he remarked "I'm taking this tram," and both hurried into the only vacant seats near the entrance of the car as it started. Neither spoke. The tram moved on until it reached Donegall Street where it stopped to pick up passengers. Two women got in. One young beautiful and attired in a magnificent fur coat with a lavish display of colour and jewellery and the other almost completely covered by a shawl.

"Oh, isn't that a gorgeous coat," whispered Miss

Bennington excitedly. Ned looked around the car and discovered there were no vacant seats. Sylvia gazing admiringly at the lady nudged his side but he looked past the forward fur-coated figure which stood as if waiting on him to rise. At the door of the car the other woman stood with her back to the passengers. A long dark well-worn shawl that hid her head and shoulders and a stained dark skirt were all one could see of her. She seemed to want to remain unnoticed and held her shawl tightly across her face.

Ned, who was the only male passenger inside the car, felt the eyes of the well-dressed lady upon him and the nudges of his companion, but reaching his hand towards the door he gently pulled the dark-shawled figure towards him and rising from his seat allowed it to take his place. Miss Bennington was seething with anger and her feelings were not improved by the obnoxious smell of the Spinning Room from the poor woman.

At the corner of the Antrim Road the offended girl was glad to leave her seat, and the sound of her, "good-night, Mister Brady," left him wondering if his lesson would have good results.

When he reached home that night the young man felt as if he had struck a blow for his oppressed people. Without him knowing it the poor dark-shawled woman to whom he had given his seat in the tram was none other than Mrs. McCann the mother of the girl Sheila.

CHAPTER FOURTEEN

Liza's Pub

"You go ahead to yer work Sally, and I'll try and lie here to dinner time," Barney Bubbles Hanna said to his wife one morning as he shot a lovely little bubble up at the ceiling. Both were in bed and the mill-horns screaming outside.

Sally tossed in the clothes. Rubbing her eyes, she whined "Bad scran to ye," and scrambled our on to the floor where she immediately knelt down to say a mouthful of prayers. In the homes of the Row the day always began with prayers. After that, the women flung on their bits of working clothes, peeped at the sleeping children (if they had any) and made a hurried drop of tea and a quicker exit.

Poor Sally Hanna was a spinner and a great woman. She could rear children, mind a husband, watch her job, keep a house, help the neighbours and still smile. Barney Bubbles as you already know, was a rougher and an entertaining fellow as well. For the fun and good nature that was in him everybody loved him and found excuses for his faults. Each morning, when Sally his wife was at her prayers and the mill horns blaring Barney Bubbles coughed. The sound of the mills was enough to start him. By that cough the neighbours on either side knew the day had begun in the Hanna household and called it the

Hanna alarm clock.

Often Barney Bubbles jokingly remarked that, "the blasted horns always brought the ploucher," but strange to say his cough was also very bad on the Sunday when the horns were silent. Peter Brady however, insisted the rougher brought his Sunday trouble on himself by spending too much time and too much money in the pubs on the Saturdays. To Barney Bubbles a pub was always inviting. At any time of the day it had its charm. In the morning it was quiet, in the afternoon sociable and at night riotous. Into any of these atmospheres he could fit, provided, of course, there was an occasional bottle. Sally did not begrudge her man a drink but never wanted him to take too much. Barney Bubbles on the other hand, insisted that was impossible.

As a home-keeping woman Mrs. Hanna was a model in the mill Rows. Her little house was always spotless. The small kitchen, the narrow scullery and the tiny rooms always proclaimed the vigour of her restless arms. On entering the kitchen the first things one's eyes were attracted to were the two shining brass candlesticks and clean delph dogs above the fire. There was a brightness about everything that made one wonder where to look next until the dresser at the side of the stairs forced its rows of immaculate white cheap delph upon you.

A large fender scoured thin and displaying the words "Home Sweet Home" then caught your attention and you found yourself wondering if it were always just like that. Only sickness in the household ever dimmed that fender or those candlesticks. That deal table near the fire had been scoured a thousand times and red tiled floor on which it stood marked down its history on Sally's back and knees. Then all the holy pictures with their gilded frames and shining glass rushed into one's eyes from the bright coloured walls. Everything seemed too near and too clean, Sally's sharp eyes rebelled at dirt.

Except for an odd house in which there might have been a delicate woman every kitchen in the Row was kept like this. To have been poor was considered bad enough but to have also been lazy was deemed a crime. Each night after her work Sally cleaned up and each day her eldest daughter of ten years attended to the other four small children and prepared the meals.

On the morning in question Barney Bubbles had not to go to work. He was free until after dinner hour so when Sally had left the house he turned in his bed and fell asleep. A few hours later the eldest daughter, when she had dispatched the other children to school, aroused him. Getting up he donned his working togs and went downstairs to his breakfast of dipped bread and tea. With nothing to do the cough was troubling him and somehow Liza's pub, at the corner of the Row, kept popping up before his mind. In the midst of a kink, he remembered his book with Liza was clear. Then a Bushmills bottle flashed before his eyes. For a short time, he dwelt on the nice label the oddly shaped bottle and the sparkling liquor, then he left the kitchen.

Liza the publican and her sister were old residents of the Row. In poverty, many years earlier they had reached Belfast and split a shawl between them. This had been their start. Having the wit to hold to what they got they were now fairly well off. Both sisters were good publicans and as soon as Barney Bubbles marched into the shop they asked concernedly about his cough.

"I'm sorry to say it's not a whit better" said the rougher taking up a position near the far end of the counter and asking for a "wee Bush".

The two sisters pulled down their black clouds and smiled as they drew near to attend to the customer. At that moment the rougher was the only one in the shop and so received their undivided attention. Being more suspicious of them when they were together he watched what bottle was being taken from the shelves. Liza was the talkative one while the other was generally described as "too deep and too dumb" some of the Millworkers actually believing that Liza's chatter was only used as a smoke-screen for the sister's tricks.

"There's little risk with the first drink" thought Barney Bubbles looking admiringly at the "wee Bush" that was left before him, "providing of course that you watch where the bottle comes from". Satisfied he had received the right article and taking a mental note of the position the bottle occupied on the shelves the rougher looked around the quiet shop and began to promise himself a few peaceful hours, and a few peaceful drinks.

Allowing his eyes to travel back to the glass before him he permitted them to feast themselves upon it until he could endure no longer. Then lifting the whiskey to his lips he was about to drink when Liza leant towards him saying in a frightened voice.

"Billy Clarke's on the beer again". "My God" ejaculated the rougher, swallowing the drink before he realised it. The shock of the news and suddenness of the swallow had deprived him of the anticipated enjoyment. He was angry. Silently he cursed Billy Clarke and Liza the publican. The later whispered again. "He's broke loose again and went out just as ye came in of the door and he's like a roaring lion".

"Terrible" groaned the quiet sister pulling at her knitted cloud. "Give me another Bush" snapped the rougher keeping an eye on the door and dreading the return of the boozing tenter. "Do ye see that?!" Liza, pointed to a huge mirror that covered the wall near the door as she spoke. "Well he wanted to break it and it took three men and me and my sister all our time to stop him, whatever notion he took".

"Terrible" moaned the gloomy sister. "Holy Heavens" added the rougher suddenly awakening to the fact that he had forgotten to watch which bottle the publican gave him his "wee Bush" from. The drink was at his elbow. He was too late of thinking and had a suspicion it was somewhat duller in appearance than the last. "It was the son Arty's fight with Shanklin that put him on the beer" Liza explained leaning over the counter.

"Jemity Moses" snapped Barney Bubbles holding the glass in his hand and examining the whiskey. He was fascinated by his problem. Good or bad he was determined not to lose the enjoyment of this glass as he had lost the last. He prepared to drink when the publican excited whispered. "Here he is!" and the door was knocked open by Billy Clarke.

Before the rougher could think what had happened the whiskey was down. It was swallowed before he had even tasted it, "To hell" was all he could say. He would have hidden but there was no place to hide and the drunk man had seen him. Putting his hand across his mouth he stifled a fit of coughing as the tenter staggered up the shop and flung his arms around his shoulders. For about a minute there was painful silence. Then the rougher's keen ears heard Liza's long-faced sister moan "Terrible. Terrible."

Tears streamed down the face of the drunken man. "I'm ashamed, I'm a disgrace, I've wrecked a happy home" he said, leaning on the rougher's shoulder.

Relieved that the strong tenter was in this humour, his friend saying sympathetically, "You're alright Billy, you're alright," made an effort to console him. Like a shot the tenter detached himself and swinging his arms began to yell defiantly in Barney Bubble's face. "Ye're a liar, ye're a damned cursed liar."

Striking the counter with such force that it shook the building he screamed angrily. The rougher was sorry he had spoken. Looking towards the door he quivered. "Give us a drink" roared the wild man. Nervously the rougher whispered to Liza. "Make it two and mark them up to me". The tenter glowered round the shop muttering to himself. The drinks were served. With watching Billy, Barney Bubbles again forgot to follow the publican's movements. When the drinks were on the counter he reprimanded himself. They looked dull. He thought, he detected a substitute for a smile on the solemn face of the silent sister. The duller the drink the brighter was that face.

Billy Clarke's eyes turned to the mirror and Liza shivered. "Here's yer whiskey, Billy" she pleadingly informed him. At the sound of the word whiskey the big tenter softened. Blinking at the rougher he squeezed our tears and sobbed. "Barney I'm a brute, I'm a no good, I'm a waster".

Almost remarking, "You're alright" the rougher checked

himself in time and remained silent. The tenter, however, was not satisfied. He wanted some reply. The silence provoked him. Hitting the counter he roared angrily, "I'm a no good, I'm a brute." Then he raised his glass to his lips.

In his own muddled head his friend searched for something to say and at last raising the "wee Bush" remarked, "Ye were always a decent man". With a bang Billy's strong fist came down again upon the counter. Yelling defiantly, "What do you know about me? You bedamned for a man" he hammered the counter and faced his friend. Before he knew, Barney Bubbles had swallowed his drink and the big man's face bursting with anger was pushed against his own.

Liza's sister, crossing herself, forgot to say "Terrible". She began praying. No policeman being near she summoned the aid of the saints. Barney Bubbles was sorry he had spoken at all. He was also sorry about the drinks he had not enjoyed. Unable to make up his mind whether silence or speech was the better in the circumstance he stood puzzling his brain. While thus engaged his drunken companion lifted an empty bottle. Waving it about his head he approached the large mirror and glowered at his own reflection. "For God's sake Mr Hanna don't let him break the mirror" Liza pleaded whisperingly across the counter. "Thank God there's a decent inoffensive man like you in the shop this morning" she added.

Swinging the bottle round and round, the drunken man shouted challengingly at his own refection. Then as if relieved by roaring, he returned to the counter where he drank his whiskey and called for two more drinks.

Still clutching the empty bottle he swayed to and from the counter while the rougher watched his hand lest a sudden fit might cause the weapon to fall upon his own head.

"Here's yer whiskey gentlemen" said Liza placing the tumblers before them and making an effort to appear brave.

Barney Bubbles forgot his friend in order to examine the publican's alleged "wee Bushes". Cursing himself for again not having kept a watchful eye on Liza's movements he spat out. About the liquor, he thought there was a sickly greenness. It was more like lamp-oil than whiskey.

"Watch him Mr Hanna" Liza pleaded, "That mirror cost a lot of money".

The glum sister continued talking silently to the Saints. She was wondering if the storm had subsided. Billy drank his glass and then roared for two more.

Disgusted with the whiskey he had received but determined to make the best of it, the rougher modestly raised his to his mouth, "We've got enough, Billy".

"Who's got enough?" snapped the tenter turning with a violent swing that knocked the rougher's drink clean out of his hand. "Holy God" wailed Barney Bubbles moving back from the counter to pick up the remnants of the tumbler from the floor and quietly cursing his friend.

While thus engaged he could hear Liza's whispering voice beseeching across the counter, "For God's sake don't let him break the mirror, don't let him break the mirror".

In his mind the rougher said, "damn yer mirror." "Give us two more" bawled Billy, but his friend looked towards the door. Having decided he had enough the rougher was preparing to go.

Another drink, of the kind that Liza was serving would leave him incapable of reaching home. Already an impulse to become violent was taking hold of him. On the other hand, Billy Clarke after the last drink was fast becoming slobbery. Rattling money on the counter he now sobbed, "I'm a brute, I'm a brute, give us a drink, give us a drink."

Hearing the rattle Barney Bubbles placed his hands over his face to watch Liza through his fingers and saw her fill two glasses out of a strange mysterious coloured bottle taken from below the counter.

"Mind the morrow, don't let him break the mirror" bleated Liza placing the drinks before them.

The tenter swallowed his without question, but the rougher sniffed at his and then closed his eyes to let it down. It tasted like paraffin. Its effect was almost instantaneous.

Billy Clarke began to roll stupidly round the shop and his friend commenced to viciously sing a wild Irish song.

> "Let the tyrant bribe and lie,
>   We'll have our own again,
>   Let them threaten fortify,
>   We'll take our own again."

To the spirit of the song the tenter tried to respond. Putting his arm around the singer's shoulders he appraisingly exclaimed, "Bully Barney" Thus encouraged the rougher continued.

Just as the song ended the mill-horn sounded. Hearing it the rougher remembered his work and his wife. Sally would soon be home. At that moment Billy Clarke lurched towards the mirror.

"For God's sake mind the mirror, mind the mirror," called Liza appealingly. Barney Bubbles blood was up.

"To hell with ye and yer bloody mirror" he shouted as lifting the empty bottle that his friend Billy had left on the counter the rougher crashed it into the cherished glass. Amidst the noise of it's smashing the two men rolled out of the shop and reached the street just as Peter Brady the hackler was passing by on his way from work. Almost tied by his drunken legs Barney Bubbles stood looking after him. He knew the strong religious feelings of his hackler friend and burning with the desire to have a fight screamed.

"There's no God Peter – there's no God." But the big hackler passed on to his dinner without replying.

CHAPTER FIFTEEN

In the Brady Home

With an enthusiasm that was intended to relieve the pain of his parting from Sheila McCann, young Ned Brady settled down to his new job. At having escaped so suddenly from the annoying attentions of Sylvia Bennington he experienced a great joy, and the few shillings of improvement in his small wages were hardly thought of. In his new office he assisted a man who having visited many parts of the world had much to communicate and Ned loved to listen. 'Chatty and kind', was how Ned described him and the young man found much to talk about when he arrived home each evening.

In the mornings the home of the Brady's was all bustle. At night it was mostly chat. Because after work many of the men dropped in to have a quiet talk and hear the news, it was called the 'Parish Parliament'. Everything of interest was discussed in the kitchen. Amongst the visitors, Mrs. Brady, always pleased with the company, moved like a spirit. The neighbours knew she liked to see the house crowded at night. It was company for her two men.

After he had his tea and a wash-up, Peter Brady always took a race up to the chapel where he said a few prayers. This was followed by his usual dander towards the hill. Then he hurried back to the company. About eight o'clock young men of his son's age and a few older generally arrived to take their seats around the fire. Football, politics, religion, work, etc. were discussed.

One night, some time after Ned Brady had started in his new job, the Brady fireside was surrounded by men. In the course of conversation someone referred to the Moran family next door. In the Row the Morans were unpopular, but it did not seem to worry them because they had big notions and no desire for popularity with their own class. The Morans had made up their minds to escape by hook or crook from their surroundings and were ashamed to be known as a hackler's children. A family of three young men and three girls all of whom had secured jobs in the offices or shops downtown, they hated to touch shoulders with or even recognise the shawlies. At their door beggars were afraid to call and no neighbour ever thought of asking them for the loan of a spoon. Even the wild birds that came to the streets for crumbs on Sundays never lingered near their door.

"That stinker doggie Moran passed me by today in Donegall Street without speaking," complained one of the young men addressing his remarks to Ned Brady. Another remarked jokingly, "I suppose ye had on yer da's patched trousers and that cap with the holes in it." Everybody laughed. The first speaker however was angry. "I was covered with towe and could have found my heart to rub myself up against the brat," he continued.

Ned looked at his young friend and explained, "Ye needn't cry. All the Moran family are like that. They wouldn't even recognise their own da if they met him in the town because he is a hackler. Why Arty Clarke says one of them told a girl he met that their da was of independent means and they never admit they live in the Row."

"And hadn't to do such a filthy thing as hackle," mimicked one of the young men.

There was a general laugh after which someone said, "What a shame and the poor oul' da slaving twelve hours a day for the past forty years to bring them up."

"Sure, they can't help that" began Ned Brady stoutly. "Mr. Plover who is in my office and who has travelled the world, says the system we live under is to blame and that it makes people dung in their own nests."

"What kind of a man is he with a name like that?" asked a chap in the corner. Ned was delighted to get speaking about his overseer.

"He's very learned," he began, "he has been in many countries, can speak several languages and has read a lot. He believes that the people who are good are the easiest to exploit and he says the fellow who has a soft heart is a mug for this system."

"He must know a thing or two Ned," someone remarked. "Yes," replied Ned, "he says the poor cherish virtue, but the rich are too busy cherishing their riches to bother much about it. He believes that the way of living that's forced on us is no way at all for people who are good or want to be good."

"That man's not far wrong Ned," coughed an old rougher, "when ye see how the bad people get on in this world and the good ones go under, it makes ye think. As far as I can see the way of living that's on us is only for making the poor poorer and the good bad, it doesn't seem to have any other purpose."

A young hackler took up the thread, addressing Ned Brady he thoughtfully began. "Perhaps that explains why the Morans next door are hard Ned. They had good parents and saw how they were slaved and how their goodness was taken advantage of and so may have decided to leave the slaves and get in with the slavedrivers."

"Does he ever say anything about Ireland?" asked Paddy O'Neill.

Paddy always wanted to hear something about his country, and like many of the young men of his age believed if Ireland got Home Rule the poor would no longer be poor.

"He does, Paddy," answered Ned, "and he thinks this island contains as many fools for its size as any other country, look at the mugs the English people are. They own about a quarter of the world and with the exception of a few thousand their millions are as badly off as us." "But," persisted Paddy, "what does he say about the great men like Emmett, Tone and the others?"

"Oh" answered Ned, "he says the great men fought and died to relieve the oppressed people but he thinks a good many of them didn't even know what was oppressing them. Even today he contends that some of the leaders think a green flag without a crown waving over College Green and an additional penny a dozen on the eggs for the farmers, would solve our problems. In the South they think we Northerns are awful people as if people who have to slave under frightful conditions so as to provide cheap linen for the world could retain all the virtues of the fresh green fields and the fresh air."

Paddy O'Neill was dissatisfied. He moved restlessly on his chair. Another question was on his tongue as a rap came to the door. Ned Brady shouted, "Come in."

The latch lifted, the door opened, and into the now smoky kitchen stepped Father Mick. Everybody stood up. Mrs. Brady carried a chair from the scullery for his reverence. Placing it before the priest she rubbed it carefully with her apron saying respectfully, "Ye're welcome Father, yer very welcome."

On the priest taking his seat all the other men resumed theirs. The young clergyman looked carefully at each face. He then asked. "Where's Peter?"

Mrs. Brady looked at the clock and apologised for her husband's absence. Ned however, assured his reverence that his father would be back shortly. Deciding to wait, Father Mick resigned himself to a chat with the company. Nobody wanted to deprive the priest of the honour of leading off so there was silence for a few moments. This was at last broken by Father Mick pleasantly remarking. "I hear that this house is called the Parish Parliament and that they call Johnny's Box the Upper House."

Paddy O'Neill who loved to get talking to a priest edged forward in his chair.

"Aye Father," he began, "it's just like the Rosehead and Arthur's Rivers. The young lads learn to swim in Rosehead and when they think they know enough to keep them floating they go up to Arthurs."

Thus, reminded of his young days an old rougher stirred in his seat and joined in. "It was grand Father. It was grand when ye were able to dive below the wee stone arch at Rosehead and come up to the other side. Ye thought ye were no goat's toe when ye could do that."

Father Mick laughed, "We only take to the depths when we have spurned the shallows," he explained adding, "I suppose the lad who was able to dive through the Rosehead arch was qualified for Arthurs River, touching the bottom too often can breed contempt."

Paddy O'Neill still had his country in his head. Poor Paddy. All his people were very poor. Starvation and empty pockets, however, had not destroyed his courage. He had a good heart and strong broad shoulders and thought if he could lift the big men of his own country up, he would lift his own people. For the ten years, since he left school, he had worked hard to help his family, but his miserable wage was swamped in the effort. For him it appeared an impossible task so Paddy had pinned his faith to the green flag and had a kind of foolish conviction that if it were raised it would never soar over poor people. Older men than himself had thought that way and the belief was passed down like red hair.

"What do ye think about Home Rule, Father?" he anxiously asked. Looking at the lad's earnest face the priest quietly answered, "I'm afraid Paddy talking alone will never get us that far." "Hear, hear Father," applauded Ned Brady. Ned had decided opinions of progress and was quite hot as he spoke, "Ye only get crumbs by begging and only get mercy by crying. It's not crumbs and mercy the poor people want. It's their own and they should prepare to take it."

The priest was shocked. Lowering his brows, he spoke with deliberation, "I'm afraid you misunderstand me, Ned. When I say talking alone will never get Home Rule, I mean we should use prayer."

The men looked knowingly at Ned Brady. The lad was perplexed. Having no desire to offend the priest he stopped himself saying that *putting guts into the poor people would be better for them than resignation to slavery*, but felt he must say something and so asked, "Do ye think, Father, that God expects the poor to do nothing else to relieve themselves but talk and pray?"

Father Mick frowned. Replying in a voice tinged with anger, his face grew red, "I'm afraid Ned you are learning too rapidly." This, particularly before his pals, nettled the young man who somewhat heatedly asked, "Is it a bad thing to learn? Is it a bad thing to become angry at seeing good people tortured? Is it a bad thing to see their pleading and praying abused? Are good people to be always hounded into factories and mills and measly houses and kept in pious starvation?" Having said this Ned felt more confident.

"My dear Ned they are good because they are poor," quietly suggested the priest, "They are driven closer together in their affliction."

Mrs. Brady moved near her son and plucked at his coat. She dreaded him saying anything to offend the priest, but Ned had himself under control and a confidence in this own strength was manifesting itself.

"Ye say they are good because they're poor," he drawled,

"but surely hunger and slavery aren't the best things to make good men and women."

Father Mick looked towards the lad's mother and seeing her flushed face and look of anxiety remarked, "Look how the poor cling to each other. Look how the fathers and mothers cling to their children. They have no wealth or property to cling to, so they cling to each other." The men were silent as the priest continued, "In my short experience I have found a death more painful to the poor than to the rich and a joy a greater joy. Their poverty my dear boy can make them better- make them good and remember God weighs burdens before he sends them." Ned smiled. "If ye believe that why don't ye denounce riches more, why don't ye say it's a sin to have them?" Ned was struggling to retain control of himself. Watching the interested faces around him he spoke as if angry and disgusted, "for the poor people that we know there is only hell on this earth."

For a moment there was silence, then an old rougher dryly remarked: "Next stop Heaven," but the priest fixed his eyes on Ned.

"When you grow older and have more experience you may see things differently and learn to take them as they come," rising from his seat he added deliberately, "with the pinch of life that is all around you I don't blame you or anybody else for squealing and I am with you all in your grumbling."

All eyes bent towards the fire. Everybody wondered if his reverence was annoyed. Priests were so touchy. Mrs. Brady who had escaped to the scullery, was trembling and praying for her boy. Securing his hat Father Mick remarked "I'm sorry I can't wait any longer on your father," and was standing in the centre of the kitchen when a stone crashed through the window against the linen blind. Pieces of broken glass rattled on the floor. Those near the window jumped from their seats and the voice of a man in the street was heard screaming.

"Send him out, send him out. I can beat the best man in the Row."

The priest's face paled. Mrs. Brady entered the kitchen. All eyes were on the window. Then from the street came the roar of the same voice this time shouting, "To hell with the Pope and Peter Brady." "God save us it's Barney Bubbles on the beer again," said Mrs. Brady.

"We're in for a lively night of it," remarked her son as the mother turning apologetically to the priest remarked, "It's too bad, Father, for this to occur and you here."

It was evident that the priest felt uncomfortable. Ned's conversation had annoyed him, but the drunken affair was more embarrassing.

"Does he get drunk often?" he asked. Everybody smiled as Ned Brady replied, "About every six months Father, and when he does, he wants to fight."

In the street the voice still roared, "To hell with the Pope and Peter Brady." "Isn't that annoying," said the priest, "what on earth put him on the beer?"

Somebody laughed as an old rougher explained it was old Liza's mirror. The priest did not understand. Outside the drunken voice continued to roar, "To hell with the Pope and Peter Brady." This time the noise of a scrimmage followed by cries of 'murder, murder' were heard from the street and a rush was made to the door. Pushing, with the others, his reverence was in time to see the man he had come to visit, Peter Brady, taking off his coat and squaring up to the drunken rougher in the centre of the street. Women and children danced with glee around the fighters. People stood at every door and as the noise increased others came running down the street. Nobody backed Peter. Everybody shouted, "Go on Barney Bubbles," and roared with laughter.

Pandemonium reigned in the Row. The priest felt out of it. With swinging arms Peter Brady made mad rushes at Barney Bubbles driving him back. Then the rougher, with his head down, charged stupidly at the hacker's stomach. Seeing that Mrs. Brady not merely smiled but made no effort to restrain her husband Father Mick concluded she was a callous woman, but what surprised him more was that young Ned Brady sat laughing on the windowsill while his father danced and fought in the street.

The priest was busy thinking how to get away as quickly as possible from the hysterical crowd. Amid the cheers and laughter of the wild people he at last took his leave hurriedly and hastened up the street. As he reached the top of the Row and was about to turn into the big road a hurrying old man asked, "What's the matter down there yer reverence?" "A fight," answered the priest recognising the man. "Who's fighting?" the old fellow asked. "Peter Brady and Barney Bubbles," said the priest making to stride off but pausing at the hearty laugh of the old man. "Ha, Ha, Ha," he roared, "Peter Brady and Barney Bubbles. Have ye no sense at all? Ha, ha, ha, ha, Peter Brady and Barney Bubbles."

Father Mick stood in bewilderment until the man's spasm had abated. Wiping the tears from his eyes the old fellow still beaming asked, "Did Barney Bubbles break Peter's window?" the priest nodded. The old man laughed again. "Did he shout to hell with the Pope and Peter Brady?" The priest said "Yes." "Ha, Ha, Ha," roared the man "and did Peter take off his coat and square up to him?" he asked.

Again, the priest said, "Yes." After which, between his laughs, the old man said, "Why yer reverence that's what happens every time Barney Bubbles goes on the tare. They're two great friends they love each other, and they come from the same part of the country and Peter just strips off his coat and pretends to fight him. After he has Barney Bubbles tired out, he carries him home and puts him to bed, Ha, Ha, Ha."

"Strange people," said the priest to himself as he left the old man and continued his walk towards the old house.

CHAPTER SIXTEEN

Mr. Polver

> Dear Mr Brady,
>
> I was expecting you to call to see me last week but as
> you didn't. Perhaps you will drop in tomorrow as I have
> something of great interest for you.
>
> Yours till a cinder,
>
> Sylvia Bennington

This letter, written on a scented coloured paper, was delivered to Ned Brady one morning almost two months after he had left the Bennington office.

On his way to his work, he re-read it. The scent, the 'something of great interest', the 'Mr. Brady', annoyed him, and he tore it into small pieces during the walk towards the town. Ned had no desire to see Miss Bennington again. To even think of her was a bad thought. He was convinced everything that was beautiful in a girl was in Sheila McCann's possession, and that Sylvia Bennington was possessed of a devil. When he thought of Sheila he thought of birds and flowers and heaven. When he thought of Sylvia he thought of sin. In his mind the impoverished stuffy home of the McCann's had been made beautiful by Sheila's presence whereas, the large, gardened residence of the Bennington's was defiled by its contact with Sylvia. Yet, he was angry with Sheila, or was it that he was painfully disappointed.

On the day he had sat with her on the heather of the dark hill above Johnny Connor's the girl had promised to write him 'a big, long letter' as soon as she had arrived in New York. Two months, during which he had feverishly waited and prayed passed, but no letter reached him. To add to his pain others in Ravage's Row had read him communications they received from her. For some reason he could not understand, no letter came to him and Mrs. McCann's answers to his anxious questions about her daughter seemed cold. Then he noticed the McCann's children passed him without speaking and Father Mick, who formerly used to joke him about the girl, had ceased referring to her when they met.

America changed people, Ned had heard of boys and girls being changed there.

Ravage's Row was a poor place and in rich quarters poor places were easy forgotten. Sheila's Aunt Margaret was rich and the people, whom the girl would meet would also be rich. Sheila was pretty and they would laugh at the thought of her having anything to do with a poor hackler's son, and few girls could defy those laughs. So thought the lad yet he longed to hear from the girl and tried hard to believe the absence of a letter was due entirely to his late arrival at the boat on the night she had sailed.

In the office, that day, his far-travelled senior, Mr. Plover, was in a new humour. His talk began with women. The assistant had hardly sat down at his desk when the learned man opened the discourse with, "To be a good wife, a woman must have a vocation, she must be made for her job."

Ned smiled at his handsome friend who continued, "My woman's no blooming good. She wasn't meant to be a wife at all, she doesn't know the first thing about it."

The younger man was surprised. This was not like Mr. Plover who was always so courteous to women. Something, thought Ned, must have upset him that morning. The senior dipped his pen in the inkpot and adopted a different tone of voice, "Of course, Brady, I don't blame her, in fact I blame myself. My wife in all fairness to her, doesn't relish being a drudge, and a wife to me could not possibly be anything else on my mangy earnings." Ned listened and thought of his senior's six pounds per week and how happy Sheila McCann and himself could be on it.

Mr. Plover wrote in the ledger that lay open before him and talked. "It's blooming strange though. My own mother had a vocation or two vocations for wife and mother. She could endure anything when she believed it was for the family's good. She could make any sacrifice for the home. She was a perfect slave and fitted in, with her four children and man, to a twenty-one shilling's a week scheme of things- but it was a blooming tight squeeze."

Plover laughed as he looked at his young friend's serious face. "Look here Brady," he said, "you're young in the world, you have plenty to learn, watch good mothers. They're strange things. Everybody else goes out after reward but they don't seem to ever think of it, yet they give the most of all. My old woman gave us of her best. "She had some reward from you and yer brothers," interjected Ned who was thinking of his own mother. Mr. Plover lowered his voice. There was an expression of pain on his face as he replied, "Not at all Brady. She had no old age. She passed out quite young. She gave all she had to give and then collapsed before anybody could give her anything. I was a young fool. I was away in Africa when she died. No word ever reached me, but I was getting older and out there beginning to appreciate her. When I came back, I had presents for her in my trunk and castles in my head. But it was too late, she was dead and buried."

Ned Brady thought he saw a tear on his senior's cheek and sympathetically remarked, "She must have been a good mother." "Good," said Plover sharply, "God help your mother Brady if she's one of her kind. They suffer plenty but suffer so silently nobody knows. Amongst them, no matter how terrible the burden, the greatest crime is to whinge. They endure in silence till they smash."

As his friend talked, the patient slaving mothers of Ravage's Row came before Ned Brady's mind. He saw them smile though hourly tortured by their inability to give their little ones all they were entitled to. At least, he thought, if they were prevented from providing the young ones with sufficient food and clothes, nothing could stop them from lavishing on those children what they could give of generously namely, their love. The thought of how those poor mothers loved their little ones actually pained him.

Mr. Plover continued, "They're just good slaves, just good slaves, they don't kick in their chains, they kiss them." "But," he declared with emphasis, "The woman I got for a wife's not like that. Mine kicks like fury against drudgery. She refuses to take on that end of the job and by gum she gets far more out of life. She doesn't ask for herrings and get herrings; she demands salmon and leaves the herrings for whoever wants them.

Plover laughed loudly and turning in his seat looked at his young friend, "If you ever get a woman, Brady, it's doubtful which of the two kinds will be the best for you in this get-up-or-get-under world."

Ned had already made up his mind what kind of a woman he wanted, and his conclusions were summed up in this remark: "I would like her to be like my own mother". This was said with great earnestness.

Mr. Plover knit his brows. After finishing an entry in the ledger, he again turned towards his friend and made a dramatic gesture, "But surely, my lad, you wouldn't like her to have to live as your mother lives or to endure all she endures."

This remark set Ned Brady thinking. He often thought of marriage and when he did, he thought of Sheila McCann. Now he was asking himself would he like to see the girl having to live as his mother lived. Could he, he wondered, ensure for her a better living?

Before he had time to answer these questions for himself his talkative friend had again spoken, "Every blooming fool of a slave thinks of castles when he thinks of his girl and forgets there's never enough castles to go round until both of them are in the sink together."

Ned was pained. He pictured the homes in the Row and stammered, "But, - but many of them be happy."

"Happy, be blowed," shot Mr. Plover, "If they were less happy, they would be less miserable. They kid themselves that the sacrifices they have to make are only for one another when they are actually used to strengthen their exploiters hold and weigh their chains. To make their paltry wages be sufficient they eat less and console themselves they're starving for each other, when they're really starving for the boss. This world, Brady with its scrum for riches only wants mugs like that, and even then the squeezers are sorry we eat at all. Nothing would please them better than to discover a way to keep horses and workers without having to feed them." Then bitterly he added "But a day will come when the scoundrels will be sorry and that will be when the workers won't be able to use up all that in their greed for profits they have got them to produce and the day of reckoning follows."

When he talked in this vein his young assistant was thrilled. To no subject did Ned Brady respond more readily than the cause of the working people. To him Mr. Plover appeared to know so much about their conditions and see so clearly that he had come to regard him as their champion. His senior could tell of how black, yellow, and white were slaved in countries he had visited and could describe the brutality of their enslavers.

Ned Brady was seeing the world through Plover's eyes. "It's a great pity your church doesn't denounce this system of robbery for that's all it is," Mr. Plover remarked, "It's a pity they don't come out more on the side of the poor people?" "But they do," stammered Ned, dreading what his friend was going to say about his church. "No, they don't," said Mr. Plover, "they are like ourselves, so much in it they compromise. They point out where the individual or individuals are wrong whereas it is the whole system that's immoral and that makes the individual bad and not the individual who makes the system bad." Deciding he must say something, Ned thought of the early masses and the shawled congregations at Ardoyne and said, "Our church does welcome the poor, our church is packed by the poor." Mr. Plover grinned broadly. "Yes Brady," he remarked dryly, "it's like all the other churches it welcomes them and requires their money, but does it concern itself enough about how they sweat for it or if they get any at all for all the sweating. We ourselves don't do enough about it so, it can't be wrong to think the churches don't do all they should about it."

This remark stirred the Catholic in his assistant but merely stating that rich and poor were alike in his church, Ned bit his lip. However, his silence did not appease the senior who angrily shouted, "The system makes the rich and makes the poor, the rich don't need to be lifted out of torture, but the poor do, and my view is that the churches should denounce the system that's making such unfair divisions of Gods bounty."

"But," asked Ned quietly, "is that not a matter for the people themselves the churches care is for souls you might as well expect the church to fix a sewer pipe as to expect it to fix the way of living we've made ourselves." This appeared to calm Mr. Plover who dropped his head into his left hand and grunting, "Perhaps you're right, Brady." And proceeded to silently concentrate on a tot in the ledger.

Pondering over all that had been said the young man

continued his work. The conversation was at an end. The clock ticked. The pens scraped. Then suddenly an attractive woman very well dressed, swept into the office. Ned, who was nearer the door, rushed to attend to her only to be confronted by a raised chin and outstretched arm that pointed at Mr. Plover as a confident voice said, "I want to see him." The young man stared. The woman's cool confidence stunned him. In the Mill Row she would have been described as a cheeky hussy. Something told him this was his senior's wife and turning from the counter he saw Mr. Plover grinding his teeth and leaving his seat.

"What the devil brought you in here?" asked the husband angrily, showing no pleasure at seeing his wife.

How terrible, thought Ned, for anyone to speak to a woman in that way. In Ravages Row no husband would be so impolite to his wife unless he were drunk. He would have liked to have closed his ears. "Don't be angry, darling," drawled the woman soothingly, as she stretched out an open hand and added, "I need some money badly dearie, and please do give me as much as you can."

Mr. Plover cursed. "Damn you," he said, "Do you think I'm made of money; you seem to think of nothing else but money." The woman smiled very sweetly, "I wish you were, dear, I know of nothing better to think of." Fumbling in his pockets the angry husband extracted two sovereigns. These he flung on the counter, "That's all you're getting, that's all I can give you." The lady gathered up the money gracefully and with a broad smile and a, "You're a sweet, dear" sailed out of the office.

Ned Brady held his head down as the door closed and

his senior resumed his seat. "That's what you get for marrying out of your class," said Mr. Plover.

"That wife of mine belonged to what they call the upper class and they don't suit marrying at all. Some of them think it's only a poor man's pastime. They regard it as a joke or a means to an end whereas the poor regard it as a divine institution. The poor man's ambition's to have children better than himself but the rich think no one could be better than them. I was born in a slave family, but that wife of mine was a slave-driver's daughter. Slave driving's in her blood."

Ned thought of Sylvia Bennington. She would be one of the same kind, he decided. Mr. Plover continued, "Hell mend me. I should have known better. I had thought her class better than my own and got what I darn well deserve." Watching the handsome face of his friend the young man smiled. His senior continued, "Those blooming women are too fond of freedom to be pinned down to the gridiron and the washtub. They hate what your mother and my mother had to do. To them a slaving wife's work is only a fool's job," Then looking cutely towards his young friend he said strangely, "But they're good stuff to play with, Brady, particularly if you can afford it. They don't die of broken hearts if you leave them and when you tire of one it's a good thing to get another. Some men take to drink when they get a woman like my wife. I don't. It costs too blooming much, so instead of drinking I get a fresh one of the same kind and have fresh fun."

This shocked his young friend who loved to think of women as angels. Ned was in the act of saying something, angrily, when he remembered how Mr. Plover cherished the memory of his own mother and so he checked himself. Then his mind flew to Sheila McCann, and he found himself wondering if she would ever change.

As both men continued their work the remarks of the elder man lingered long with Ned, to whom a greater surprise awaited at the end of the day for when he left the office after his senior that evening, he was astounded to see Mr. Plover with Miss Sylvia Bennington linked closely on his arm, enter one of the hotels on the way home.

CHAPTER SEVENTEEN

In Billy Clarke's

Ravage's Row always thronged with poorly clad children, but for several years the children of Mrs. McCann had the distinction of being the most poorly clad of all. About three months after the eldest girl Sheila, had arrived in America this was changed, and the family suddenly became the best dressed in the Row. New pinneys had arrived for the little girls, suits for the boys and all of them actually wore boots. This transformation caused much talk amongst the neighbours whose children commenced to whinge for boots and clothes they could not get. In fact, as well as being responsible for bringing widespread unrest amongst the little ones it brought pain to many of the parents. However, all the neighbours were pleased with the change in the McCann's fortune and, if some expressed the hope that it would do them no harm, this was sincerely meant. Even the home of the fortunate ones spoke of better times. A window that for years had been stuck together with paste and paper, was replaced by a new one and the two front windowsills of the house painted a bright yellow.

On his way up and down the street Ned Brady noticed these improvements, but he was particularly struck by the elder children's refusal to answer him when he addressed them. Their mother, he also noticed, had left the door when she saw him coming up or down the street. Perhaps, he thought, it is a case of what Mr. Plover had so often described: "In leaving their poverty they were leaving their class."

Around the district the workers talked about the grand job Sheila McCann had got in America and about the loads of clothes and dollars she was sending home.

"That's the only way we'll ever get clothes for our children," many poor parents concluded so other young people were made ready for America.

Meantime Ned Brady was losing hope of ever hearing from his girl again. The months passed by and the changes in the girl's family became more manifest, but no letter reached him. The promise she had given to write on arrival remained unfulfilled. That the United States and her gaudy Aunt Margaret had proved too many for her was Ned's first conclusion.

What galled him most, however, was that one of the boys of the Moran family who lived next door had received several letters from her and boasted about it.

Luggy Moran, as he was nick-named was a prig of that priggish family. He was the very last person Ned would have expected her to have written to. At no time had Ned ever cared for him. To the lads of the district Moran was a "stink-pot." His uppish airs and offensive manner were family characteristics; the Moran's always striving to convey they were of a superior class to their neighbours. By all, they were regarded as bosses' lick-spittles.

For Sheila McCann to have written to one of them was proof to Ned the girl had changed and changed much.

"Don't be sitting moping there, lad," shouted Peter Brady to his son one Saturday afternoon, many months after the girl had left for America. Peter, after his week's hard work was having his usual head-neck-and-shoulders wash as he sang, "For you are as fair as you were Maggie when you and I were young." The boy, home from the office, sat near the kitchen window peering through the blinds.

"Man dear, clean yerself up and go away over the hill to clear the cobwebs out of yer chest," the father shouted while stripped to the waist, he jerked a rough towel up and down his broad back as he came from the scullery. Peter, of late, had been watching his son and was becoming anxious about him. The boy had grown very quiet. Something told the father he was vexed at not having heard from the McCann girl.

Out of the corner of her eyes Mrs. Brady also watched and thought. Both parents knew their boy had received no news from America. Both feared the young girl had 'lost her head' with her well-off Aunt Margaret and 'forgotten herself'.

Rubbing his chest Peter Brady cheerily shouted, "Take a stick with ye lad and get away up to the mountain."

Convinced that her son had grown paler of late the mother approached to where he sat and said gently, "A breath of air will do ye a world of good, son, ye that does be confined so much in an office all week."

Ned, who had only smiled at his father's loud voiced suggestions, turned from the window at the sound of the gentle voice. Putting his hand on the mother's arm he explained:

"I promised to go up to Billy Clarke's ma. Mrs. Clarke stopped me on the way down. It appears Billy's coming off the beer and she wants me to give him a game of draughts to lift his mind and as an excuse to keep him in the house."

Although the anxious parents would have preferred their boy to have gone for a walk in the fresh air they, nevertheless, were relieved to learn he was going to Billy Clarke's and when the lad left the house they agreed the company there 'would help to lift him out of himself'.

Billy Clarke's house was only a few doors away and like all the others in the Row. Children were playing on the floor and Mrs. Clarke was working about the kitchen when Ned Brady walked in for his game of draughts, but there was no sign of Billy.

"Where's the big fella?" asked Ned taking a seat near the fire. Mrs. Clarke, a nervy pale-faced woman, continued her work as she replied, "He's out Ned, he's out, I wish he was in."

"Is he coming off the beer alright?" asked the visitor. "That fight of Arty's was too much for him," replied the woman. "He was too much excited by it and God help him he forgot himself. He's making a great effort to come off but this is a very bad day for him to be out of the house. On Saturday there does be far too much money knocking about and too many wanting to stand drinks."

Ned Brady agreed and sat debating with himself whether to wait for Billy or go for a walk up the dark hill. The woman proceeded with her housework.

Knowing the temptations of a Saturday Ned, after a few minutes thinking, decided to leave but as he rose to go the noise of unsteady feet came into the hall. There was fumbling at the latch for some time, after which the door opened, and two drunk men came sheepishly into the kitchen. They were Billy Clarke and Barney Bubbles. Barney Bubbles shuffled to a seat near the window and Billy sank down heavily on a chair by the fire.

Mrs. Clarke stopped her work. Her critical look fell on the arrivals. Billy appeared to be awaiting her remarks. His head and lower lip hung. The rougher half closed his eyes and pulled down the peak of his cap as if to hide himself and guard against attack.

Mrs. Clarke's examination must have been painful. Both men winced under it.

"Merciful God," she at last exclaimed addressing Ned, "Did ye ever in all yer born days, see anything like that?"

Young Brady made no reply, while the drunk men, as if relieved by hearing the sound of the woman's voice shook themselves slightly and began to move their heads.

"Where were ye?" asked Mrs. Clarke sharply addressing her husband. Billy's eyes looked towards Barney Bubbles and then towards Ned, but he remained silent.

"Do ye hear me, where were ye?" demanded the woman in a louder voice. Billy's chin fell on his chest and his eyes almost closed but there was no movement from his lips. At a hole in the knee of his trousers Barney Bubbles picked.

Having decided that she must shake her man Mrs. Clarke

was in the act of approaching him when the door opened and a woman, who had never darkened the door before, rushed in. It was Liza, the publican, and she was flushed, breathless, and excited.

"What in the name of God does she want in here?" though Mrs. Clarke, but she hadn't long to wait until Liza made her business known. Looking at Billy and his pal, the publican began by apologising to Mrs. Clarke for coming to, "annoy a decent woman on a Saturday. It would ill behove me to be intruding on ye Mrs. Clarke and I wouldn't do it, but that yer husband is just after stealing a bottle of whiskey from my shop."

"Suffering God," exclaimed the astonished wife as she stared at a picture of the Sacred Heart that hung on the wall. "To think that Billy Clarke would ever stoop so low."

Ned watched the culprit who seemed to be making foolish efforts to hide his head in the breast of his coat. All eyes were on him. There was a painful silence.

Again, expressing her apologies for annoying a good woman Liza shook her fist at the thief. Mrs. Clarke could think of nothing, but the disgrace attached to the charge. With tears in her eyes, she moaned, "God save us all, this is terrible, this is terrible. To think that my husband would steal from the likes of you and yer quiet sister, two defenceless inoffensive women. My God, how will we ever raise our heads again after this?"

From where Ned Brady sat, he was able to see the neck of the stolen bottle protruding from Billy Clarke's coat pocket. The sudden arrival of Liza seemed to have completely paralyzed Billy, but it had the opposite effect on his friend Barney Bubbles. With the intention of searching her husband's pockets Mrs. Clarke crossed the kitchen. Before she had reached him however the rougher rose and approached Liza. Addressing her in a polite manner he often effected when drunk he dramatically said, "Liza this is a severe shock to me. I am astonished by yer statement and cannot find words to express my disapproval." Then turning towards the flabbergasted Billy who at that moment was feeling his last and only friend had deserted him he said reprovingly, "Billy Clarke I never expected this from you, you have disappointed me beyond description."

Nice man, Mr. Hanna thought Liza while the rougher continued. Billy was withering. "I have known Billy Clarke intimately for a lifetime but never though he would ever stoop to anything like this. It's the meanest trick I have ever heard of. If I had thought for one moment he could have been guilty of such a doing I would never have been seen in his company, and to think he would steal from a decent kindly neighbour like yourself Liza makes me sick."

Denounced by his pal poor Billy squirmed. As if chained to the chair he sat while his friend continued to belabour him and lavish compliments on his accuser. "I always knew that ye and all belonging to ye were decent people," said Liza bowing gratefully to the speaker.

But Barney Bubbles was not finished. Pointing towards his pal he resumed, "God knows I have my faults and plenty, but stealing isn't one of them and I am pained beyond measure to think of what that man has done to a good neighbour whom we all know and love so well."

"Billy Clarke," he shouted, "if you have a bottle of Liza's whiskey in God's name give it up like a man and don't make your shame any deeper."

Standing at the tenter's side the speaker stood waiting while his stupid friend, with his chin still buried in his coat, sheepishly extracted the bottle from his pocket and handed it up to him.

Politely the rougher asked Mrs. Clarke, who all this time was speechless, to get a piece of paper. With this he carefully wrapped the stolen bottle and amidst grave apologises and much ceremony handed the whiskey back to Liza who expressing her regrets and thanks hurried out of the house.

All this time Ned Brady remained seated and silent finding plenty of amusement watching the expressions on the faces around him.

Mrs. Clarke appeared disgusted and disgraced, Billy looked disowned and despised, but Barney Bubbles eyes seemed to smile behind an angry mask and from the arrival of Liza he had sobered up remarkably.

When the publican with her recovered bottle of whiskey had left the house the silence that followed was distressing. Tears appeared on Billy Clarke's cheeks and his wife wiped her eyes with her apron. The Clarke home was shaken. Ned Brady did not know what to do or say. He felt for the poor tenter and was shocked at the rougher having turned on his chum. Billy let the tears fall and never raised his hand to stop them. Mrs. Clarke moved towards the scullery. Then after a full minute Barney Bubbles spoke. As the sound of his voice broke the silence all eyes turned in his direction. It had a different tone. It was no longer affected. Even Billy raising his head slightly opened his eyes as wide as he could.

"Have ye a corkscrew anywhere handy? asked the rougher addressing Mrs. Clarke and at the same time extracting a large bottle of whiskey from his trousers pocket. Billy's eyes brightened. Ned Brady smiled. Both realised what had happened. Barney the rascal, had also stolen a bottle from Liza's shop.

Billy Clarke made an effort to straighten himself in the chair. The thought of another drink encouraged him. Barney Bubbles was still his friend.

Ned rushed to the dresser and reached the corkscrew. Completely bewildered and not knowing whether to cry or laugh Mrs. Clarke disappeared into the scullery. A smile began to play upon the tenter's face. Watching his friend screw the corkscrew into cork his tongue moved joyfully along his lips. The clouds had lifted. With a, "Ha, ha, Billy ye should never lift a bottle of coloured water in front of a mirror." Barney Bubbles gave a jerk and pop – the cork was extracted. Then taking up a position in the centre of the floor he called for cups.

These he received and holding the bottle above his head he was in the act of proposing a toast for the occasion when the door opened and Liza the publican rushed in.

CHAPTER EIGHTEEN

The Milkman Calls

J ohnny Connor's new horse Rory had given him bother. Only by degrees had it discarded some of its upper-class manners, thus rewarding its poor owner for his suffering and patience. As Johnny said, "Having been for years a rich man's pet the animal did not take kindly to becoming a poor man's slave and like 'superior' people had developed 'superior' tastes and preferred the best roads and the easiest living." To the pavers in Ravage's Row he showed his dislike by prancing until the sparks flew. This used to amuse the children.

When Johnny and Rory arrived in the Row each morning with the milk the mountainy man's voice could be heard shouting, "whoa there Rory." To the little ones a milk-cart that had come down from the top of the big green hill was a thing of commanding interest. The dung upon its wheels spoke of the country. It had travelled far and brought sweet-milk – and milk belonged to the soft fields and the big green hills. To them the country was wonderland – Johnny's horse and cart belonged to there. As they drew near the children stretched their little necks or stood on tiptoes in efforts to secure a peep at the baskets of fresh eggs it sometimes carried and when they had called, "Good-morning Johnny," they felt their little voices had addressed the dark hill's heathery summit.

Each morning Johnny Connor was a godsend. He came down from heaven and carried good things to the Row, and the Row was Purgatory. "It's not often I see ye in the mornings. Is the work scarce this weather?" the milkman asked on being met at the door by Mrs. McCann herself.

"Holding out a blue jug for the milk the woman replied: "I wasn't feeling a bit well Johnny, so I'm taking the morning off. Give me an extra pint."

Johnny poured out her requirements and expressing the hope that the "wee rest" would do her good, asked if there was any word from her daughter Sheila lately. "Whoa there Rory," he roared as the animal pawed at the pavers.

"We had a letter from her yesterday," said the woman, "she's doing well and was asking for ye, but Aunt Margaret's very bad and it's going to be touch and go with her to get better they say."

"Do ye tell me that?" asked Johnny, keeping an eye on the prancing horse. For the rich Aunt he had no liking. "Does Sheila be homesick at all?" he asked.

Mrs. McCann rubbed her eye with her thumb as she answered, "Poor girl, she hasn't forgot about home and it's being sore with her to be so far away and so far from her own."

"I would expect that Mrs. McCann," said Johnny, "Whoa ye devil," at the restless horse. "She was a tender sort of flower to be transplanted so far away."

"She was that," replied the woman, reaching the money for the milk. Only accepting part of what had been tendered the big man explained he was not charging for the extra pint. "Ye're far too good to us Johnny," stammered the grateful woman, "but I'll say a wee prayer for ye in return if that's any use."

"That's the way – a widow's prayers go far," smiled Johnny, as with a "gee-up" he left the door and walked down the Row alongside his cart.

As Rory and Johnny moved off, the grateful widow, with a dimness in her eyes and the blue milk jug clutched tightly in her hand gazed after them. Her thoughts at that moment were of her late husband and his delicate health. The roar of machinery, the stuffy rooms of the mills, and his frail failing form came before her in contrast to the strong frame of Johnny Connor and the smell of milk and scented heather that accompanied him.

Johnny's next call was at the Moran's the uppish people, who thought themselves better than everybody else in the Row. At their door he was always addressed as Mister Connor, and he did not take kindly to it. It was a door also that had to be knocked differently from the others. They were strange people who seemed to spend their lives finding fault and it took very little to irritate them.

"They're a whinging lot," was how Johnny usually referred to them.

On this morning the eldest answered his knock, supplying the milk the hillman was about to walk off when, with a pained expression on her face, the girl lamented. "That's not very generous measure this morning, Mr. Connor."

"No Miss, there was no rain." replied Johnny pleasantly, then calling, "Whoa! there." Rory was moving away. "I beg your pardon! Mr. Connor" said the girl questionably. The milkman did not think it worthwhile explaining. He had no respect for her intelligence. Saying, "good morning, Miss," he started the horse and passed on.

With a snow-white milk-jog in her hand Peter Brady's Maggie stood at the door when he reached the house. By the sight of Johnny and the horse and cart, she was always made happy. The hillman always brightened more when he saw her.

"Whoa, there – that's a fine morning Mrs. Brady," he shouted in one breath.

"It is that, Johnny," the gentle woman, admiring Rory, replied. "Yer new horse is doing well for ye, and I hope it'll be long spared to ye."

Johnny filled the jug and looked in the direction of Moran's house. "Yer heart's in the right place anyhow," he began, "Man it's grand to meet decent people. God must have made the others just the way he made ugliness so that we might know the difference."

The horse pounded it hoofs on the street. "Whoa, there," its owner roared, then turning to Mrs. Brady he remarked, "Rory was bothersome fellow at first but he's a bit more reasonable now. I only wish I could train some of my customers as well as I can train horses."

Peter's wife smiled. She knew what he meant and when he and his cart had left her door she looked after them wondering how anyone could annoy such a good man as Johnny Connor.

After making his calls in Ravage's Row the milkman was

proceeding to the big road when he met young Ned Brady at the corner of the street. Ned was on his way to his work in the town and was in a hurry. However, he stopped for a minute and in that short time the man from the hill told him in confidence that he had received a letter from Sheila McCann. In it, he explained she had asked him to send her out a piece of heather from the hill. The mountainy man appeared to have been moved by her request-clapping his hand on the young man's shoulder he said, "Damn it, Ned, there's good stuff in her. She didn't forget the oul' hill anyhow so I sent her a sod with heather on it," Then with a knowing smile he added, "and I took the sod from the very place where you and she sat that day before she left."

To this the young man made no reply. He was made thoughtful by the news. Leaving the milkman staring after him he continued his journey towards the town.

"Silly boy," mused Johnny as, with a "Gee-up," to the horse he mounted his cart and drove across the big road.

He had not driven far when he met another friend. Near the gate-lodge of one of the mill-owner's houses he saw Peter Brady, the hackler, and after a short conversation about Rory the horse, Johnny asked his friend to come for a drive with him on his runs. Peter took a seat behind the cans, and the men continued their talk. Johnny's next call was at the home of Jasper Crumlin, a mill-owner. It was a magnificent house situated in its own walled grounds and approached by a long drive.

Except on a milk-cart or some such delivery a hackler could never get into the large gardens behind those high walls.

'Strictly Private' appeared in warning letters at the gate-lodge and on the trees. Except on business no worker was allowed to pass through that gate. It was almost a crime for workers' children to dare to peep in at the flowers.

To Peter Brady a drive past the gate-lodge and through the gardens was an adventure and something to be excited about.

By his friend's invitation he had been tempted. In his working clothes he could sit behind the milk cans and admire the beds of flowers, the short-grassed lawn, the fruit-laden hot-houses and the big house, so when Johnny had asked him to come, he jumped into the cart without hesitation. What delightful stories he had promised himself to be able to tell about all he saw. Although living in the district many years, he had never got further than peeping through the gate like the children or jumping at the low parts of the wall in order to lift his eyes high enough to catch a swift glimpse of what was inside.

Jasper Crumlin, the mill-owner was a cruel man, and the fact that he was surrounded by beautiful gardens only seemed to accentuate this. 'A friend of hell' was how he was described by some of those who had to slave for him. Others spoke of him as 'a bad breath' so to meet him on the road was considered an ill-omen.

On the way up the drive the two men sat in the cart chatting as Rory jogged along the pebbled path. Johnny was one of those who never wanted to lay eyes upon Jasper Crumlin. "I hate the look of him. I don't feel well, and things go wrong all day after I see him."

"He's a foul breath," he often said. Even his horse Rory seemed to know when Jasper was about. Drawing near the house the animal sulked this morning and the milkman whispered to the hackler, "The growler's about."

Jasper's wife and family were like himself. Amongst them it was said a good seed did not exist. Nobody, they seemed to think, had a right to live well but themselves and their friends. Workers, were expected to exist on crumbs, speak in whispers, hide in the narrow streets and doff their caps or curtsey to them if they passed by. On this morning the sulkiness of Rory made Johnny nervous. "I tell ye Peter," he remarked, "it bodes no good."

Drawing in at the back of the big house and leaving his friend on the cart Johnny dismounted to leave the milk with the servants of Jasper. Rory was very restless and scraped with his front feet at the loose white pebbles. "Steady there, steady there," Johnny called softly, but the animal tore at the ground and snorted. Peter Brady leaned over the cans to pat his rump and spoke soothingly in vain. "Steady, steady," called Johnny pouring the milk into a can held by a servant. Rory, growing more impatient continued to scatter the pebbles all over the place, disfiguring the path.

Carrying a stout stick in his hand Jasper Crumlin suddenly appeared from a sidewalk. With his very red face much redder than usual the mill-owner roared angrily. "Train your damned animal Connor, if you can't train yourself." "I'm sorry, sir, I'm very sorry, sir," said Johnny, hurrying with the pouring of his milk. "Steady Rory, steady," he called pleading to the horse. Jasper's presence, however, seemed to further irritate the animal and although Johnny called and Peter patted, it grew more vicious at the scraping.

For a moment Jasper stood glowering then approaching the side of the cart he crashed his heavy stick brutally on the animal's front legs. So astonished was the milkman by the force of the blow that he dropped the can. Raising itself on its hind legs the injured horse pawed madly at the air. Taken completely by surprise, Peter Brady, almost fell from the cart. With a smirk on his face that seemed to say *I have done something to be proud of* ,the mill-owner stood a few yards off. Pity was in the eyes of Johnny Connor, pity for the horse, then with a blaze of anger he fixed them on Rory's attacker. For a second he stared at the now almost purple face, then, like a maddened bull he bellowed "you cur" and charged towards the mill-owner. Hurling a sudden shower of smashing blows upon the face of Jasper he sent him sprawling on the path.

When the mill-owner rose from the ground blood flowed freely from his mouth and nose. With his both hands covering his battered face he ran down the drive, to be followed by the loud laugh of Peter Brady until he had disappeared into the house.

Affectionately patting and calming the wounded horse and also trying to get himself under control Johnny Connor watched the retreating figure. He was glad and sorry. Then something happened. Two girlish arms were flung around his neck, two warm lips kissed his cheek. It was one of Jasper's servant girls. Then she ran away. The hill man was amused, then turning the horse and linking his arm in Peter Brady's he led the animal towards the gate where his hackler friend left him.

On his way home to the hill that evening the milkman recalled the servant's warm lips on his face, the firm handshake of Peter his friend and the touch of Rory's nose upon his shoulder and decided he was well compensated for the loss of one customer, or any other consequences his action might have.

CHAPTER NINETEEN

A Death in the Row

T he day Johnny Connor struck Jasper Crumlin the mill-owner was a black one for the Bradys. Peter Brady, the staunch friend of the mountainy man, was dismissed from his job, the foreman explaining it was upon instructions from the manager. Peter knew why. His hearty laughter at Jasper's collapse had sounded too loud and too annoying in the beautiful silent lawns of the Crumlin domain.

To any worker the sack, as dismissal was called, meant gloom. To Peter Brady it was a terrible tragedy. For many years he had worked in the same place, and of this record he was proud. He loved to give satisfaction at this occupation. A hard-working religious man, who never had allowed his wife to slave in the mills and who toiled in the hope of saving his son from similar slavery to him, the loss of his job was a dreadful blow. Self-reliant for a lifetime, he would have died rather than have to take anything from his boy or have his wife deny herself any of the little she was receiving.

For weeks the big man wandered from mill to mill in search of work to discover the influence of the powerful Jasper Crumlin had preceded him and closed the gates. The court case that followed Johnny Connor's attack on the mill-owner had advertised the hackler's name.

Unable to secure a berth he began to lose heart. That his son Ned should have to keep him was a torturing thought.

His walks became shorter, his chats fewer and the splashing of cold water on his head and shoulders ceased.

No son, however, appreciated his father's long years of effort and sacrifice more than Ned Brady. Often, he had thought of them and vowed to make some return. To see that father in a job away from the mills he would have given his heart's blood. When his parent was dismissed he began looking around in the hope of finding such a position for him. As the weeks passed the lad saw his father become broken-hearted and listless. Without work he was without spirit. Ned searched persistently to find him something to do. One day he, at last, succeeded in securing a store man job in the town.

Overjoyed the lad could not get home quick enough that evening. At last he had been able to do something worthwhile for his good father. On his way home he tried to imagine his parent's reception of the good news and pictured to himself the smile that would adorn his mother's face. A job away from the mills! The old horse-tram moved too slowly towards the hill that evening. His happiness swelled the lad to impatience.

"Thank God, my da won't have to go back to the mills again," he prayed. How often had he longed for this day? At last, it had arrived. One of his long-cherished ambitions had been realised.

With a light spring he leapt from the tram when it reached Ravage's Row. With a song in his heart and on his lips, he hurried past the houses. His mind was too occupied to notice a change in the street. No children were playing on the hard pavers. No women stood at the doors which now were closed. The blinds of all windows were drawn. Ned's brisk step and cheery song were all that disturbed the unusual silence of the usually noisy street. Then with a light heart he entered his home. On the tip of his tongue, he carried the good news for his father.

Opening the door, he was ready to make it known but drew back. Barney Bubbles the rougher was sitting by the fire. He had his hands holding his head. Ned's eyes roamed over the kitchen and towards the scullery. Where is Ma? And what has Barney Bubbles in the house at this time of day? He wondered.

Mrs. Brady was always in the kitchen when her son arrived. Only something terrible could explain her absence. Then the lad noticed the table. It was not laid, and no kettle sat on the fire. The fender was dim and dusty.

"My God, Barney," he muttered as if to himself, "the fire's dead." "Ma, ma," he called loudly but the rougher rose from his seat and beckoned for silence.

"Don't be calling Ned," he whispered, turning his gaze towards the ceiling, and adding sadly, "she's upstairs with yer da."

It was enough – that explained all. His father was ill. The rougher's eyes were wet. He noticed that. Now everything came back to him. A few weeks previous he had heard his mother speak of headaches she did not like and several of the older men had said his father had failed terribly of late.

The lad was up the stairs like a flash and tiptoeing into the room saw his mother leaning over the bed and gently wiping the pale pained face of his father. With lips tightly closed and hands clasped in prayer, Mrs. Hanna and Johnny Connor sat near the window, and the boy thought he saw black beads in the fingers of the woman. Then his young ears caught the sound of the heavy breathing of his sick father, and he noticed that his eyes were closed.

Mrs. Brady did not require to look round. She knew her son was near and as the lad put his arm around her stooped shoulders tears fell on the patch-work quilt that covered the bed.

"It's a stroke he got this morning after ye left son," she whispered without raising her eyes from Peter's pale face.

"Did ye get the doctor?" quickly asked the lad. "We did, son, but he thinks there's no hope," the mother sobbed.

Ned was stunned. Falling on his knees by the side of the bed he burst into tears and prayers.

When the doctor had failed, '*it was only God that could succeed*' was how he thought, and the strength of this praying shook his strong young frame like an ague.

The mother dried her tears. Turning to Mrs. Hanna, she asked her to go downstairs and make a drop of tea for her boy. Mrs. Hanna understood. Mothers talk with their eyes. Taking a reverent farewell look at the sick face on the pillow, she passed quietly down to the kitchen where she put on a fire, laid the table and soon had the kettle boiling.

Between the gasping breaths of the dying man the song of the kettle below crept into the room. On the mantel board the clock ticked.

Muttering prayers for the dying Mrs. Brady bent towards her husband. Her son sobbed beside her. From his chair by the window Johnny Connor stared at his dying friend. The hillman's lips moved. From below came the voice of Mrs. Hanna.

"Come down for a drop tea, now, Ned," she called mother like. "I want no tea, I want no tea," cried the son, shaking on his knees.

"Poor boy," murmured Johnny. Gradually the sobs of the lad died down. In the kitchen below someone had removed the kettle from the fire. Its singing ceased. Only the heavy breathing and the tick tock of the clock remained. Peter Brady was sinking fast. The minutes passed and with their going his breathing grew weak. The sound of the clock grew stronger. Tick, tock, tick, tock. Now and then, Johnny Connor cast an angry glance towards it. His ears were strained to follow the fading breath of his friend. Tick, tock, tick, tock continued the clock, its sound increasing to provocation. Leaning forward from his chair, Johnny strove to catch the fleeting breath. Had it ceased? Was he gone? He asked himself.

Had the footsteps of his friend's breath passed on? From the bed, silence, dead silence was coming. Now like the bang of an enormous hammer tick, tock came from the clock. There was a slight movement on the pillow Johnny strained to hear. The breathing had ceased. Mrs. Brady dropped quietly to her knees. Tears came to the hillman's eyes. Rising from his chair he stopped the clock. Ned Brady cried beside his mother. In the kitchen Mrs. Hanna and Barney Bubbles began to pray. They had heard the clock stop. Then the hillman pulled down the window to let the soul of his friend pass out of the small stuffy room and as he did so he could not help recalling the often-repeated expression of his departed friend, – *Next Stop Heaven*.

CHAPTER TWENTY

In the Bereaved Home

"P eter's only away a wee while before the rest of us," said Johnny Connor consolingly. He was calling at the Brady home one night after the burial of his friend.

"I just dropped down for to help to break the loneliness for yerself and yer mother," he remarked addressing young Ned Brady, and taking a seat by the fire.

"We're always glad to see ye, Johnny," said the young man affectionately, "you've been a great comfort to us in our trouble." Mrs. Brady, who had been darning, got up from her chair. Bowing invitingly to the visitor she moved towards the scullery. "Poor Peter," drawled Johnny, "any home would be bound to miss him, he was a great spirit, he was so heart-some, he was the grandest man in the whole district."

"He was just too good, far too good – far too good for this world. Look at how he denied himself of everything," lamented the son.

"Nonsense, nonsense lad," remonstrated the man from the hill, "ye'll never understand how much real happiness yer father got from being able to do without something in order to give it to yer mother and you. His greatest ambition always was to keep ye both from the mills and he succeeded and that made him very, very happy."

Ned sat down beside his friend. The man from the hill continued. "Many's a time yer father talked over things with me. Many's a time he told me how good God had been to him even though the mills had never treated him well." "He was terribly fond of ye, Johnny," said Mrs. Brady, coming from the scullery and approaching the fire to put on the kettle. "No more fond of me than I was of him," answered the hillman proudly. "In all my life I never took to anybody as I took to Peter Brady. It was like love at first sight and we were fast friends for well nigh forty years."

"Do ye remember the first time ye met him?" asked Mrs. Brady, a strange bright look coming to her dull eyes. "Deed and I do," smiled the big man, "It just seems like yesterday, you and he were courting at the time and were going up past my house to the heather to sit and look down at the town and he was singing, 'I wander today to the hills Maggie'." A smile danced on the hillman's face as he proceeded, "and then he introduced you to me by saying, 'this is Maggie' and that ye were his girl and we all laughed," Johnny sighed and shook his head.

"Them were the good oul' days and ye were a fine young man then, Johnny," said Mrs. Brady.

Ned and the mountain man smiled at the mother's remark and Johnny continued to regale them with stories of happenings in the days gone by. The small table had been pulled into the centre of the kitchen. Tea was made ready for the welcome visitors. Mrs. Brady was always busy. Ned Brady looked at his father's friend and thought of the big hill. The men sat down to tea. "Ye must be very happy away up in yer cosy home on the top of the mountain," the young man droned. Johnny gulped down his tea, rubbed his lips with his hand and answered, "I wouldn't swap thon wee bit of a place of mine for the best mansion ye's have in the town. Sure, there's no air down here for big people never mind for wee childher or delicate ones, and God never intended childher to have to play on dirty streets and hard pavers or in entries and dung pits. To tell the truth I'm always heart glad to get back out of the din and smells and smoke so as to hear the birds again and breathe a drop of fresh air."

"My da loved yer place Johnny," remarked Ned. "He did that, he did that," the hillman began proudly, "nothing would have pleased him better than to have been able to have had a home for you and yer mother up there on the mountain."

A figure passed by the window and entered the hall. Two nervous coughs and a timid knock told it was Barney Bubbles. "Come on in," called the young man. The latch was lifted. With cap in hand the rougher entered the kitchen. "Are ye alright again Barney?" asked the hillman thinking of the rougher's last booze.

"Don't ye think it's blooming near time?" smiled the visitor taking a seat near the window. "My oul' woman's pocket and my own credit can't stand much of a spree."

Johnny and Ned laughed. "I just called in to keep ye's company for a wee while," the rougher said in explanation of his visit. "Thanks Mr. Hanna," Mrs. Brady remarked, proceeding to poke the fire, "how is Mrs. Hanna?" she asked. "Poorly enough," the rougher replied, "she' always sick after one of my spasms."

"And no wonder," drawled Johnny. "Ha, ha," laughed the rougher, then suddenly sitting up straight in his chair, with a serious expression on his face, he remarked, "but there's great excitement and goings on a few doors up." "What about?" asked the mountainy man. "Did ye not hear?" queried the rougher looking towards Ned. "No, Mr. Hanna," the mother answered quietly, "we hear nothing now since we haven't Peter anymore."

The rougher hesitated. He was undecided whether to explain or not. Then recalling what he had heard about Ned Brady being thrown over by Sheila McCann he began, "The McCann's are all excitement about a letter that came from America today. Their Aunt Margaret it appears, has died and left Sheila a power of money and there's talks about her coming home and about her going to be married to the Luggy one of the Morans." "It's lucky for the McCann's," said Johnny.

Barney Bubbles coughed, "they'll become like the Morans now. There'll be no standing them. Money always makes stinkers." "It sometimes does that," added Johnny. The rougher moved uneasily unfolding a closely guarded secret he lowered his voice to say, "and they say Sheila's coming back soon." Ned Brady picked up the poker and poked at the already poked fire. His mother began clearing the table. "They say she and the Luggy Moran fellow have been corresponding with each other ever since she went away. He must have had his eye on the money."

Mrs. Brady looked at her son but said nothing. Johnny Connor noticed the subject of conversation was unwelcome. He knew Mrs. Brady believed the McCann girl had turned her boy down, but Johnny had always liked the McCann's and had a special liking for Sheila. He dreaded saying anything that might hurt the feelings of either Mrs. Brady or her son Ned, but his affection for the McCann's released his tongue and looking towards Barney Bubbles he protestingly remarked, "Sheila McCann will be far changed if she ever has anything to do with the Morans, or anyone like them and I'll only believe it when I see it."

But the rougher was not to be silenced and quickly replied. "America has changed a lot of people." "But," remonstrated the hillman, "the McCann's were never lickspittles. They never failed their own at any time and I don't believe one of them would ever touch a Moran with a forty-foot pole."

Barney Bubbles was preparing to reply when the kitchen door opened, and his wife entered. Smiling to Mrs. Brady she began, "I just dropped in for a wee minute." Then her eyes rested on her husband and the smile left her face, "I thought ye were to go up to the Chapel to take the pledge and then go to confession" she said, with anger in her voice.

"So, I did, so I did," replied the rougher looking uncomfortable. "And did ye take the pledge?" Mrs. Hanna asked probingly. "No," stammered the husband whereupon his wife screamed, "What!" "Let him explain," pleaded Johnny Connor knowing the rougher was good at excuses. "Billy Clark and me went up together," he began "and Father Mick wasn't hearing. He's away on a mission and there was a strange priest in the box." "Well?" impatiently asked the angry wife. "Well," answered

Barney Bubbles, "Billy went in first and when he told he had been drinking ye could have heard the roars of the strange priest outside the box, so I made off as I can't ever bear scolding."

A dark figure passed by the window, on its way down the street. It was that of Father Mick and Mrs. Hanna recognised it. Taking a deep breath as if to keep herself back from collapsing the infuriated woman looked disdainfully at her lying husband and with a bitterly toned, "God Almighty forgive ye Barney Hanna," opened the door and left the house.

CHAPTER TWENTY-ONE

Ned and Johnny

After the death of her hackler husband Mrs. Brady increased her praying and a little lamp burned before a picture of the Sacred Heart in the Brady home. When she had Peter on earth she gave him untiring service. Now that he was dead, she would give untiring prayer in the hope that it would be of service to his soul. Day and night she prayed and day and night her strength grew less and less.

After the loss of his father, her son, Ned, threw himself into his work and made up his mind to redouble his attachment and kindness to his widowed mother. Resolutions showed themselves upon him. He would make the tiny home brighter for her, he would bring her many things. He would save enough to take her to the country place where she was born and had spent her childhood. Yes, yes, he vowed, that would be what she would like most. He would keep it a secret. He would save, and in the summer take her there for two long weeks. From this thought he built happiness into a pyramid. Often, as a boy, he had heard his mother talk of the wee house on the brae and the fairy thorn, that no one dare injure, outside the door. Often had he asked her to describe it.

The wee loanin' that turned in from the grey road, the

big hanging trees that dipped down to the thick yellow thatch, the green fields that seemed to creep up, up, to meet the white-washed walls and the blue hills far, far away. In his mind the lad long carried the picture his mother nursed in her heart. Ned knew the names of all the places where she had played as a girl.

He had often watched her eyes when she spoke of them, and seen the happy thoughts dancing beneath her lashes, he did not need to see the spots to know them. His mother's voice had dressed them in colour. He knew the brae face where the fairy-horn was sounded in the harvest evening. He knew the blue moss, where at the close of day the fairies played strange music in the deepening mist. He knew the brackeny field where the little ones used to look across the stone ditch in the hope of seeing a tiny fairy ride away on a large-winged bracken and he knew the lady finger knowed that was the wee-people's favourite meeting-place.

In the summer, if God spared him, he would bring his mother back there to lift her heart and ease her loneliness. How happy he would be to watch her eyes feasting on those long-separated paradises, to see her pluck blackberries in the moss and pull flowers on the big brae field. With such thoughts he threw himself into his work and prayed for his departed father.

Although much occupied the young man did not fail to notice his senior in the office was paying increasing attention to Miss Sylvia Bennington. Almost every evening Miss Bennington stood in the street waiting for Mr. Plover to leave the office and, arms linking, the pair marched off together. Whispers passed from department to department and rumours succeeded until one Saturday morning when Ned reached his work, he was astonished to see the Managing Director busily engaged in the office going over papers and pulling out drawers. "Brady," he asked as soon as Ned appeared, "can you take over this dammed fool Plover's work?"

"I will try sir," promptly answered the young man standing a short distance off hoping for some explanation. In a fury the Director flung books from one desk to another. He was angry. Turning quickly, he shouted rather than spoke, "This blasted fool Plover has made off with Bennington's daughter and is away to America. He sent me this letter last night confound him."

Foaming at the mouth he picked up a letter from the floor. Then checking himself he said somewhat soberly. "I came down here early this morning fearing something might be wrong, but I can find nothing. Everything seems to be in order."

"Mr. Plover was a very honest man sir," muttered Ned pitying his run-away friend. "But evidently a dammed fool, a dammed fool," snapped the Managing Director then approaching the young man he commanded. "Meantime Brady, you are to take over his work, you are to go into everything and report to me. We shall advertise for someone for your own job and later on fix up about salary." With this, he grabbed his hat and shouting, "I'm off to breakfast," hurriedly left the office. "Poor Plover," Ned mused to himself taking the seat at his senior's desk.

What about his wife he wondered then he began thinking of the advance for himself. How please his mother would be and how easy it would now be for him to take her to the country.

All that day the lad, in an effort to give his best attention to his work battled with his thoughts and when he had reported to the Managing Director that everything was in order and was told by him his salary would be increased to £15 per month he could have almost kissed him.

To Ned this was a fortune. Used to little he could now get much. He saw his mother smile, he saw her better cared for, saw the home more comfortable, saw her holiday materialising, then, as he wished his father were alive, a pain caught him. Anyhow he would hurry home that evening. The good news must be rushed to his mother. Good news – then he remembered the day he had hastened with good news for his father only to find him dying. No, he would not hurry home, nor tell anyone of his advancement, not even his mother. Having thus decided he walked slowly from the office that evening and after his tea sat pondering on the happenings of the day.

Mrs. Brady noticed the quietness of her son and imagining him paler that usual encouragingly remarked, "That's a lovely night Ned, and ye should go for a walk up the hill to Johnny Connor's. It will do ye good, ye that are confined so much."

As she spoke Ned fancied he heard, *'I wander today to the hills, Maggie'*, the splash of the water in the scullery and the voice of his father calling out, *'sling a lot of cowl water on yer head and go away up to the hill'.*

To please his mother and as he thought to please his departed father, the lad took a stick and set out for the big mountain without washing his face lest the splash, splash of the water might bring back painful thoughts to the mother.

Johnny Connor was busily engaged fixing a shed when he at last reached the cottage on the top of the hill. "Man dear," the big man called out at the young man's approach, "is that yerself, Ned? I'm more than glad to see ye, and how's yer poor mother keeping?"

"Poorly enough Johnny," the young man replied, sitting down on a big stone near the end of the shed. "It's a change she needs the poor soul," continued Johnny, "A change she needs. She stays in that wee house far too much and it's neither good for man nor beast to be locked up inside for long. She rarely leaves the place. The only time I ever see her out is at Mass on a Sunday morning and at my cart when I'm delivering the milk. Sometimes Ned I be tempted to stop the horse further from the door so as to lure her out, then I think a pity of her poor feet on the big pavers."

Ned knew his mother was confined too much. She had always been a home-woman. She always found something to do inside the house, cleaning, sewing, darning, knitting, scouring, preparing meals, and for a rest she knelt down and prayed.

Johnny also knew and remarked, "To serve and pray is all she asks for in life, to serve those she loves and pray for everybody – that's yer mother, boy." "That's just her," said the young man thoughtfully, as the man of the mountain continued. – "Sure, I know her kind only too well, Ned. They call them angels down in the mill Rows and God knows there's plenty of them there, but the damnation way of living that's on us is doing all in its power to break their hearts and destroy their virtue."

To punctuate his remarks Johnny hammered a nail into the shed. Bang, bang, bang, sounded the hammer while he bawled to his young friend, "Not a bit of wonder their men pelt each other with stones sometimes. No wonder we have riots now and then, for the poor people are driven half mad by their conditions." Then stopping to rest he added dryly, "Ye don't catch the highly paid fellows at a game like that, they just sit in safety and comfort and laugh at the hungry fools."

Taking a long breath, he resumed his work. Bang, bang, bang went the hammer as between the bangs his young friend from the town tried to say, "It's a pity of the poor people. It's a pity they fight with each other and are so misunderstood."

"Misunderstood be damned!" snarled the hillman, hammering wickedly at a stubborn nail. "Nobody should misunderstand them. The working people are slaved and held so tight from six in the morning till six in the evening in those filthy mills at dirty and badly paid jobs that even fighting is a welcome change. Anybody who knows anything about the mills and the people knows that even a riot is a welcome relief for the poor workers."

Ned Brady agreed, "Yes Johnny, ye're right about the mills the trouble mostly originate from them." Throwing down his hammer the hillman picked up his saw and began testing his powers on a tree trunk. "That's true," he grunted, "workers' troubles seem to always start where the crumbs are fewest, and the chains heaviest and then spread to the other places."

Johnny swung back and forward as he continued, "Sometimes I think the poor people, God help them, imagine they are relieving themselves when they are slaughtering each other and think they are breaking their chains when they are breaking each other's heads."

The young man watched the movements of his friend's strong, sturdy body. "Do ye think Johnny, the poor people will ever get enough sense to unite and fight for themselves and their families?" he asked.

The man with the saw suddenly straightened, leaving the tool sticking in the log he wiped the sweat from his brow as he answered, thoughtfully, "God send the day soon and sudden. The poor souls know they have wrongs to right but don't quite understand them, and there's too many cute fellows to tell them tholings good for them. They feel the pinch and plunge and kick like a horse, but only injure each other as they don't know what to plunge and kick against. Driven mad by the rattle of the machinery, the smell of the mills, the misery of their conditions and the cries of their hungry childher, they can only do mad things yet, but believe me boy, there'll come a day when they'll be enlightened."

The speaker sat down on the log and changing the tone of his voice, looked straight at his friend as switching from the subject, he asked with grave concern, "But tell me, Ned, what about this wee girl of yours that's in America?"

Taken by surprise, the lad lowered his eyes. The colour came to his face. Then looking towards the hill above the house he fixed his gaze upon the spot in the heather where he had sat with Sheila McCann before she sailed from Ireland. "What girl do ye mean?" he asked absently.

"Ye know damned well, wee Sheila McCann," snapped Johnny, closely scrutinizing the lad's face. "Ach," sighed the young man searching the heather, "that's a thing of the past, Johnny."

But the hillman had not finished. He loved both Ned and Sheila and his mind was made up. There was some misunderstanding somewhere. Determined to unravel the problem, although he saw the lad did not wish to prolong the conversation, he asked, "Is it true that she never sent ye a letter?"

Withdrawing his gaze from the hill, Ned Brady looked into the eyes of his friend and quietly answered, "Yes."

A thrush on a tree close by began to sing, a robin hopped across the yard and the two men sat silent. For almost three minutes they sat thus, then Johnny rose slowly from the log and grasping the handle of the saw said, more to himself, than to his friend, "Well, I'm blessed if I can understand it, for she was a good girl and came of good stuff."

All around the hill the song of the thrush sounded and the little robin, as if encouraged by the music of the saw, and the sadness of the men hopped nearer.

Ned Brady did not know whether he liked the sight of a robin or not. Every time he saw one he thought of Sheila McCann and as he was trying to forget her he endeavoured to keep his eyes from the little bird.

The silence of the men was at last broken by the hillman, "Tell me Ned, was it true what I heard about you and the Bennington girl keeping company?" "NO," came promptly. This reply appeared to satisfy Johnny who pushed and pulled as he talked, "I believe ye lad, yer a son of yer father, I believe ye, but there has been a terrible lot of talk about you and her."

Ned looked far over the hill and thought of his father who had so often and so gayfully trod those winding paths that twined away into the darkening sky. A cough from the hillman made the robin rise from the log and dart to the bushes where the thrush was singing. "They tell me that Luggy Moran is corresponding with Sheila McCann now," remarked Johnny questioningly. "I wish him luck," Ned sharply replied.

Again, the lad fixed his eyes on the heather above the house. The mountainy man looked at the young man's grim face and gave a grunt, "Luck be damned, luck's a fool and pluck's a hero." Then straightening himself up to his full height and staring at the lad's steady eyes, he asked seriously, "Are ye going to let a brat like Luggy Moran pluck a rose like Sheila out of yer very hand?" He added, "If you do, Ned, ye're not made of the stuff of yer father."

His young friend just shook his head. As the hillman spoke he thought of how the McCann's passed him by in the street, of how Sheila who had promised to write to him, had not written, of what the neighbours had said about her writing often to one of the Moran's and recalled all the stories he had heard of girls having changed in America. He wanted to hear no more so leaving his friend he said apologetically, "I want to bring a bunch of heather down to my ma, so I'll go up and gather it and if ye have a dozen fresh eggs and a print of butter I'll take them back with me when I'm going."

"Alright my lad I'll have them ready for ye when ye come

back," grunted Johnny. Leaving the log, he stepped across the yard as his young friend climbed up the hill behind the cottage.

Ned Brady's widowed mother loved heather. In fact, she loved anything that grew in the fields. Even a green weed received a welcome in her poor home and was placed in an honoured position. To her daisies, buttercups, and pea-the-beds were more than beautiful. They reminded her of her early country home. Heather reminded her of Peter, her late husband. He had loved the mountains and for many years had carried bunches back to her to brighten the wee house in the Row.

Ned remembered how much joy his mother had got from those bunches. He would follow in his father's footsteps. As he pulled the heather from the dry brown earth, he imagined he heard the soft voice of Sheila McCann sounding near him. The thrush sang below. A loud neigh from Johnny's horse recalled the loud laugh of his cheery father on that bright day when the lad and lass had sat together. He felt lonely. In that short space of time his father had been laid in his grave and the girl was three thousand miles away. Down in the town the young man could almost forget the girl but here on the hill he found it impossible to escape from thoughts of her.

A richly blooming heather top suddenly attracted his attention. His mind travelled to his mother, "What a lovely bunch!" he exclaimed, "How she will love it." Then he pondered on his mother's lot in life and as a vision of her struggling years passed before him, he found himself trying to probe the past in an effort to discover what things she never had and would have liked. Strangely enough his mother's wants were few.

His father's pay had been small. A dark grey shawl, a little white altar for the house and a visit to her early country home were all he had ever heard her wish for. Resolving that she would have these, he gathered until at last with his arm full of purple heather he glided towards the cottage.

"Here's yer eggs and butter, Ned and watch them," commanded Johnny Connor, reaching him a small basket when he arrived at the cottage door. "Yer mother loves a banty's egg, so I put one in specially for her," the mountainy man added kindly.

The lad took the basket and with a hearty, "Thank ye, Johnny," set out on his walk down the steep hill to the town, while the hillman stood looking after him and thinking how like the father was the son.

At every step along the road Ned Brady battled with thoughts of his deceased father, his mother, and Sheila McCann. The loose white stones on the rough road had often moved to his father's strong feet. How often had his parent trampled on them through the years? Even in his sweet hearting days he had brought his mother along that way. Mother always loved the hill. A bird flew from the bushes to the right and immediately the girl that Ned had brought that way came up before him. To chase her from his mind he tried to visualise his father's life. How as a boy he had come to Belfast to work and slave, how he had met his sweetheart, how he had married and how he had guided the home – and died. Wrapped in these thoughts the lad walked down the slope until the sound of the Angelus bell told him of the time and made him think of prayer.

After visiting the Church where he offered up a prayer for the repose of his father's soul he proceeded down the broad steps and into the big road to discover people rushing here and there in great excitement.

"What's the matter?" he called to a man who ran past. Breathlessly the man answered, "They're murdering each other down at the mills," and ran on. "Who?" called Ned after the hurrying figure. "The Catholics and Protestants," shouted the man without turning his head. Instantly Ned thought of what Johnny Connor had said, and with a prayer in his heart muttered, "Poor soul, he should have shouted back 'the working neighbours'."

CHAPTER TWENTY-TWO

The Riot

A riot was in progress when Ned Brady came down the broad road after saying his prayers. Poorly clad people were racing towards the scene of the conflict at the corner of Ravage's Row. Seeing the excited crowds and hearing screams in the distance the young man decided to go home by the back way, so crossing the and road scaling the wooden railings he entered the fields. As he tramped through the long grass he could hear the shouts of men, screams of women, and the crash of broken glass. Looking back towards the high hill he saw it had become black. As he walked he thought of the peace and quietness of Johnny Connor's mountain home up near the sky. Reaching the railings at the far side of the field he also climbed them, and at last arrived safely in Ravage's Row with his eggs, butter, and priceless bunch of heather.

The transformation in the street amazed him. No women sat chatting or knitting on the doorsteps or windowsills. There were no cheery children playing scotch-hop, or skipping, and the marble-pitch was completely deserted by the men. Like wild animals, girls, who had loved to skip and sing, were clawing up stones from the rough street and in the work were assisted by the children, while gentle women who had suddenly become mad used their shawls and aprons to carry the stones to men who were now engaged in fighting desperately at the head of the street. Protestant workers charged furiously on Catholic workers and the Catholic workers charged at the Protestants. As if both classes' lives were not miserable enough they strove to make them more intolerable. Stones, bottles, and sticks showered into the Row to be collected added to and flung back with increasing vengeance at the attackers. Provokingly, poor girls on one side of the big road screamed, "To hell with the Pope." While those in the Row yelled back defiantly, "To hell with King William."

This added fuel to the fire and attack followed attack as the daring of the rioters increased. Both mobs wanted the men who could break the most windows or break most heads. In the mills there was poor pay and no praise, but in a riot, there was much applause and therefore much 'showing-off'. What matter if your stone destroyed the fading eye of a poor old hackler who had spent himself in rearing a family on his miserable pay, so long as a few half-witted, half-starved doffers clapped you on the back.

Sides had been taken and the foolish workers imagined they were fighting for the Pope, or King William, as if either of these distinguished men would have fought with each other, or even solicited such aid if they had. To Ned Brady it was all too painful, and as he reached the door of his home and saw the genial Barney Bubbles and kindly Billy Clarke rushing frantically into the thick of the fighting, he felt a pain in his heart.

Mrs. Brady, who had anxiously awaited the return of her son, had the table laid and his tea ready. Ned saw that his mother was nervous but after giving her the bunch of heather and basket, he sat down without making any comment. The purple heather appeared to have lost its purpose.

From outside came the sound of crashes and screams. Everybody in the Row seemed to be up at the top of the street. It's strange, thought the lad, that nothing lifts the minds of the working people of Belfast from the torture of their conditions so effectively as a riot. The abandonment with which they threw themselves into it was proof they felt they must do something more than merely slave. Fighting in the streets, he concluded, was to them a nobler occupation than rotting in the mills.

The pity, he thought, was that they fought each other and not for a common cause. Poor misguided souls they imagined the road to relief and freedom lay across each other's dead body.

At the first news of a riot the poor people had fled from their small scantily furnished homes, into the street. Sewing, cooking, darning, skipping, marbles and even praying, were forgotten in the game of fighting. For the Pope and King William as they imagined, they were at each other throats while the rich were holidaying at Bangor and thinking how they would make more money out of the fighters, when they came back to work after the restful weekend. No wonder Johnny Connor always said the workers of the South of Ireland would never understand the workers of the North because in the South they never had to work in Linen Mills.

"Oh, thank God to see ye home safe. I was fearing ye'd be caught in the fighting," prayed Mrs. Brady. Then reverently fixing the heather she poured out her son's tea.

"What on earth kept ye?" she asked quietly. Ned awoke from this reverie and with an assuring smile explained, "Oh, I was just talking to Johnny Connor and on my way home called in at the church to say a mouthful of prayers for my da."

As he spoke the yelling outside increased, and hurrying feet sounded near the door. Mrs. Brady's eyes were fixed on the window. Her son saw her pale face grow paler. "What on earth is it, Ma" he asked. "God save us all son it's poor Billy Clarke away past. His head's all blood, and they're taking him down home," answered the mother, staring into the street with tears coming to her eyes. "God forgive them that hurt the decent man" she added almost bitterly. The screams outside grew louder.

"It's not the first time for Billy to stop a stone with his head, no stone-throwing contest's ever complete without him," the son remarked dryly. Then he thought of his late father and knowing that, if he had been living, he would have rushed into the fighting said to himself, "Thank God my da's far removed now from all this."

Speaking to his mother he asked. "Isn't it strange that the Protestants think if they killed all the Catholics, they would be happy, and the Catholics think if they killed all the Protestants they'd be free whereas Mr. Plover used to always say that Sandy Row and the Shankill Road were the best tonics Catholic Ireland could have, and that the Pope should pay for them a commission. In other words, ma, they render the better service to the Pope than King William and don't know it."

"Don' talk like that son," Mrs. Brady remonstrated.

"Alright ma, but when ye see poor people deluded its difficult not to be angry," replied her boy.

Just then wild screams sounded near the house and pandemonium reigned in the street. Crash followed crash as the small cheap often-cleaned windows were smashed. "They're in on us, they in on us," yelled someone and the scurrying down the Row increased. On the walls of the houses the crack, crack of stones resounded, and a mad stampede approached the door.

Suddenly an excited poorly clad breathless man burst in, it was Barney bubbles the rougher. "For God's sake get us Peter's gun, get us Peter's gun?" He panted as with flaming mad eyes he looked pleading at Mrs. Brady. "They're in on us they'll murder us and Billy Clarke's split," he impatiently added.

Ned Brady looked at the rougher and angered by the intrusion said coldly, "Ye'll get no gun out of this house if I can help it."

"You mind yer own business," snapped the rougher. "Yer da had the gun, and it was always out in the riots when he was living."

"Well, it won't be out in this row," said Ned firmly.

"Good God," shouted the rougher, "Would ye sit there and see us all murdered and a gun lying rusting beside ye." Ned crossed his legs as he answered calmly, "Listen Barney, I'm not going to help workers to murder each other and ye're going to get no gun out of this house."

"Hell roast ye for an upstart, Peter Brady's gun was always in the street when there was trouble," screamed the rougher, as looking towards Mrs. Brady he slammed the door and rushed back into the street.

When the angry rougher had left, Ned resumed his tea. Outside the screaming grew louder. For almost two minutes the lad sat eating and thinking. Then a noise in the yard made him turn his head. As he did so he was just in time to see Barney Bubbles climbing over the yard wall and dropping into the entry at the back with the coveted gun in his hand. In the yard, near the wall, Mrs. Brady stood, and the young man knew she was praying. Jumping up from the table the son rushed to his mother and catching her shoulder looked at her puzzled face as he said questionly, "My God, ma, what did ye give him that gun for?" Tears fell from the woman's eyes as she sobbed. "It was theirs son, not Peter's, it was theirs son, not Peter's. Peter would have been out with it, Peter would have been out with it, it would be Peter's wish."

Putting his arm around the frail woman he led her back gently to the kitchen. "It would be Peter's wish" she sobbed. Raising her eyes to scan her son's face she added. "They would have cursed ye son, they would have cursed ye. I did it to save ye."

"And someone will be killed just to save me," murmured Ned thoughtfully. As he put his mother in a chair a report of a gun rang out and screams rent the air.

"God stand between everyone and harm," prayed Mrs. Brady.

"My God," exclaimed her son.

CHAPTER TWENTY-THREE

Johnny Connor Calls

The riot at the corner of Ravage's Row ended almost as quickly as it had begun but left a lot of talk and bitterness behind it. A rougher and hackler, of different persuasions, were killed and several other workers badly injured. Six small homes were wrecked and many articles, the inhabitants had sweated long to buy, destroyed.

The two deaths caused no anxiety to the better-off class. The killing of two of their well-cared-for–dogs would have mattered more.

Thinking about the sad conflict made Ned Brady sick, but he could not keep from thinking. It was all so puzzling. In peaceful times Catholic workers, if hungry would ask bread from Protestants workers and get it, and vice versa. In sickness and family trouble workers always forgot their differences to help each other. Poor Mrs. Johnston sat up for weeks with poor sick Mrs. O'Donnell. Poor Pat shared his last bob and crust with poor Billy.

Knowing this and more Ned Brady was convinced the persistent torture and painful insecurity of the people's conditions made them riotous, and their lack of knowledge was responsible for the adoption of silly causes a good many of them didn't know what was oppressing them, Mr. Plover had said they were far too unselfish and too willing to fight and die for anybody but themselves. Naturally the young man believed if the workers were delivered from their brutal slavery, insecurity and poverty they would be a splendid people. His friend Johnny Connor had often said the poor people wanted to be good, but the torturous condition would not let them and Ned himself was old enough to have discovered, in the system of living, there was actually a reward for badness and many had been driven that road.

Indeed, it often pained him to think any force of circumstance could ever have influenced his angel mother to hand over a gun to a maddened man. But then even some clergymen, who started their mission well had gradually become influenced by the order of things and one part of their congregation was told to be proud of its poverty whilst the other was lauded to the skies for having escaped from it. The more he thought of the fighting the more restless he became and so for relief he switched his thoughts to his care for his mother. In his attachment to her he found peace. Here, at least was one human being whose lot he could improve and to whom he could bring some joy, and he meant to make her very happy.

The dark grey shawl she had dreamed of was at last hers. He had bought it in the town and carried it home himself, but although in the house for almost a week the new shawl had not yet taken the place of the very old black one across the grey head. On complaining about this the only reply he received was, "Son dear it's far too good for to be wearing every day." The day he brought home the new shawl his mother had smiled and patted his hand but when the snow-white altar at last arrived in the home she was flushed and so excited that she kissed his cheek and wept.

At the side of the kitchen opposite the window the altar was carefully placed and on it was laid the wee red lamp that had burned in the Brady home ever since the head of the family died. "Doesn't it warm the house son? Asked Mrs. Brady, reverently admiring her present. "When ye are at yer work and I have the house to myself I can say a wee prayer there for you and Peter."

Ned was happy, the new grey shawl might have been warmer than the old one for the thin shoulders, but the altar had warmed the home. The poor mother liked to think she could do more than just prepare meals for her son and so she often prayed before it. Anyhow the altar pleased her and that was the purpose of the purchase, so Ned was rewarded. In a short time she would receive another surprise. Her boy would take her away to the county of her childhood for a holiday. Meantime he saved, and when the winter past he had accumulated enough to defray the expenses of the promised holiday for his mother and himself.

That winter was long and cold, bringing with it many changes, while Ned Brady saved, his friend Johnny Connor on the hill had lost his delicate wife. In the month of November she had grown weaker and eventually succumbed to pneumonia leaving her husband and only child to battle on.

Throughout the long months, the young man had still secretly mused the hope of receiving a letter from Sheila McCann, but none came. People who had news were reluctant to make it known to him. So he heard nothing about the girl.

In the spring of the year the health of his mother failed rapidly. Almost daily the doctor called but the ailing woman grew weaker and weaker. Vexed at beholding the thin light almost lifeless frame of the hackler's wife, kind neighbours were heard to say, - "It's only the fear of her boy being left alone that's keeping the life in her."

In spite of her weakness, however, the poor woman refused to lie down. Persisting in attending to her household duties she struggled out of bed at the sound of the first horn each morning and was last to leave the kitchen at night. To all her son's remonstrance's she merely bleated, "Oh, I'm alright son, I'm grand, I'll be alright, you'll see, I'll be alright in a wee while," but her boy knew she was far from alright.

Broken-hearted by the loss of his own wife and over laden with sympathy for the ailing mother and her son, Johnny Connor of the hill found consolation in frequent nightly visits to the Brady home. To rest his own mind from the thoughts that haunted him in his cabin on the mountain, the big man came down often to the house in the Row where he choked his own trouble with the weight of his friends'.

A brightness came to Ned Brady's dull mother when he called. By their friends' 'dropping down' the son saw his parent's mind 'lifted', and he was thankful. Even in the mornings the big hillman was mindful, giving as much time to the sick widow as he could with the milk, and having a smiling face and cheery word prepared for their meetings.

On his nightly visits Johnny talked of hens, ducks, crops, cows, and things of the country. Though long separated from them these were the subjects the widow loved to hear. Other men who called generally talked of flax, pieces, berths and politics. The man from the hill brought with him all the freshness of her early days most of which, if not all had disappeared in the smoke and stench of the Mill Row.

One night in the early summer Johnny was leaving the Brady home. After bidding a kindly good night to the sick woman he asked the son to accompany him part of the road. The two friends were walking up the broad road when the hillman, who had been quiet, said gravely, "They say time's a great healer, Ned, but I'm afraid yer mother's never going to get over the loss of yer father."

The young man shook his head, "She's not as well as I would like to see her Johnny, and I know she never forgets da. She never lets him out of her head for a minute and she's never done praying for him," he explained.

Both men lapsed into silence. At the high trees near the top of the road Johnny stopped suddenly. Taking a deep breath and raising his shoulders as if to make a wall around him the hillman spoke with emotion.

"Ye know Ned I needn't tell ye I have always liked yer mother. She has always been such an understanding soul and ever since I met her as a sweethearting girl with yer father we have been close friends, we have been like brother and sister."

His lips trembled and he paused to steady himself before continuing, "It hurts me to see her fading away before our very eyes and to think we're not doing far more to try and save her. I'm older than you Ned and more knowing and I've a feeling ye're not going to have her for very long, the strong spirit of your father is stealing her away." The speaker wiped his eyes and looked up at the trees.

"What would ye recommend me to do about her Johnny?" asked the lad earnestly.

The hillman had steadied himself and replied quickly, "I know ye're more than kind lad. I know ye're as good a son as God ever made but yer mother needs something to lift her mind. She needs a change. It's only a change will help her, and she should be made to take it. She should be dragged away from her present surroundings and dragged quickly."

The young man, then and there, took his big friend into his confidence and revealed to him about the holiday he had planned for the month of August. Johnny listened to the story of his plans but when it was told gravely remarked, "My good lad, don't postpone it to the month of August. Take my advice and give her a change as soon as ever ye can otherwise she'll get her last change before it."

The tone of the mountain man's voice frightened him. Ned had seen Johnny Connor in many moods but tonight his message seemed unlike him. He felt all his castles collapsing around him. "Do ye think it's so very serious as that?" he asked with blind hope.

"Serious," replied Johnny gripping his arm, "Why Ned, she has been on my mind so much of late that I was going to ask ye to insist upon her coming up to my home for a while. It would do her a world of good, and she always loved it."

"Of course," he continued, there's no earthly use of me asking her for I've asked her twenty times already, and she always puts me off."

The young man knew how his mother loved Johnny's home. He never forgot the pleasure it gave her to look up and admire the wee white cottage on the big dark hill each Sunday morning on her way to mass. Often, he had heard her muttering affectionately, "Johnny's place is next to Heaven, it's so close to the sky," while at her work in the kitchen.

Resolving, come what may, he would take Johnny's advice and give his mother an early change of surroundings. Ned parted with his friend about half-way up the steep white road to the mountainy man's cottage. On his way back the young man walked briskly, now and then humming a bar of a song to help his thoughts. Reaching the bend turning into the broad road thoughts of Sheila McCann came with the humming. What was that his friend Johnny had once admonishingly said to him? "What's worth having is worth fighting for."

He was in the act of crossing the big road when a shower of stones followed by yells of, "Hide the gun!" and, "Yellow Ned," made him stop. The sudden onslaught and sound of voices came from the darkness beneath the high trees on the far side of the road. Ned felt his left leg sting from the blow of a stone, but the yells of "Hide the gun," and, "Yellow Ned," stung the spirited lad much more. For by, he had recognised one of the voices and its owner was the one person in the world he most despised.

Recovering quickly from the shock of the unexpected attack the lad turned and with his arm raised to guard his face from a further fusillade dashed across the road to where a group of young men of his age were congregated. In the centre of the group stood Luggy Moran, a sneering smile upon his face. Without a moment's hesitation Ned Brady gripped him by the throat, and before he could protect himself, dragged him to the centre of the road.

Once there, Ned slung him from him and with a fierceness that was unusual shouted, "Put up yer hands Moran and we'll see who's yellow."

"Go on – go on," came from the group of lads who began to form a ring on the road and cheer Moran. Hearing the shouts other people came hurrying to the place of excitement. In a moment the fight had begun. Like an avalanche Ned Brady flung himself at his opponent raining blows in fury on his face and body. Unable to hold his ground Moran reeled back before the force of the attack. Shouts sounded from the watchers and many men came hurrying up the road to be in time to see Luggy Moran being mercilessly battered to the ground. There he lay holding a bleeding mouth while his wild assailant stood over him. As the hammered man showed no desire to rise again his conqueror adjusted his clothes and pushing his way through the crowd strode down the road, to be followed by hurrying feet and a wheezy cough, "Ned, Ned," a wheezy voice called.

Slackening his pace the victor was joined by Barney Bubbles, the rougher, so much out of breath that for a while he could only say, "Good – great- good – yer a good 'un."

To help his friend the young man walked slower and Barney Bubbles regaining his breath asked, "What was the row about?" Still burning with anger, the young man replied stingingly, "He called me 'Hide the gun' because I wouldn't hand you up my father's gun on the night of the riots."

"Hi Ned," called another voice as the old rougher Sam Parkinson came hurrying behind the men. "Let me shake yer hand boy," the old fellow pleaded stretching out his knotted fingers. "Yer father and me were always great friends and I'm proud of ye for licking that stinking brat of the Morans."

Ned shook his hand and with a rougher of a different religion on each side of him continued his walk down the road. "Hallo Barney, how's the cough this weather?" asked old Sam on discovering Ned's companion was Barney Bubbles his fellow rougher. "Much the same as ever, Sam," answered Barney Bubbles. "How's yer own?" "Ah it troubles me most at the night-time," lamented his aged friend. "And how's the wife?" asked Barney Bubbles. "Poorly enough, poorly enough," droned Sam, continuing sadly, "She's never been the same Barney since our only boy was shot in the riots down the road. It was a sad day that for her and me Barney." The old man sobbed.

Ned Brady saw Barney Bubbles turn pale and there was a sad silence until they parted with the old man at the corner of the row. Without speaking the two men walked down the street and Ned thought he saw tears in Barney Bubbles' eyes as he left him at his own door.

In the home Mrs. Brady was waiting in the kitchen when he entered but the lad was so upset by his trying night and painful thoughts that he immediately knelt down at the white altar and prayed for old Sam Parkinson and his wife – and Barney Bubbles Hanna.

CHAPTER TWENTY-FOUR

The Mother's Holiday

As the days passed Mrs. Brady's praying increased although her health continued to fail. She refused to rest from her household duties. Neither priest, doctor nor friend could induce her to remain in bed after the early mill-horn had sounded. Each morning the sick woman struggled up the road to early mass, returning to prepare the breakfast for her son. In her attention to her son, she was painstaking and continuous. Nothing the lad could say or do, however, could persuade her to rest. Even his friend, Johnny Connor, who continued to call often, had pleaded in vain.

The hillman's stories of ducks and geese and things of the country were now losing their power to brighten her. Her face grew paler and body lighter.

"A change, a change, she must have a change," the doctor urged. "It's only a change will lift her mind," insisted the priest.

Ned had spoken to her about going to the country to only receive an impatient and pained, "No, no, no," in reply. When he suggested a few days with her friend Johnny of the top of the dark green hill, she just went on with what she was doing and muttered, "Talk sense, child, talk sense."

As the lad watched her failing frame he was disheartened, but his friend Johnny, being older and having more 'understanding' than himself knew it would only be by force or strategy that the ailing mother could ever be given a change, and he soon suggested a plan whereby that might be accomplished.

On the afternoon of the second Sunday in July the weather was beautiful. On a walk to the top of the dark hill, Ned Brady set out from the Row.

"I'm going up to see our friend Johnny," he informed his mother as he gently splashed the cold water over his face in preparation, and found himself humming quietly, "I wander today to the hills Maggie." "Alright son," his mother replied.

When he had gone the ailing woman knelt down before the white altar where, from an old prayer book that had once been her husband's, she read the prayers for the dead. Outside the little children played on the street and women sat on the doorsteps to enjoy the sun. For over an hour the praying woman knelt in silent communion with her departed husband when the door opened quietly and Mrs. Hanna, carrying something below the end of her shawl came into the kitchen.

"I just came over to see ye and bring ye this wee drop of beef-tea, it will do ye good," the rougher's wife said after she had deftly closed the door and produced a dark jam-pot from beneath her shawl. Taking a chair close to where the widow sat the woman stirred the liquid with a spoon and then reached the pot to the sick woman. At first Mrs. Brady demurred but the persistence of her friend at last made her surrender.

"Ye're too kind, ye're far too kind Mrs. Hanna," she bleated. "Not a bit more kind than yerself," replied the rougher's wife. "Many's the service ye brought me and mine and it would be ill behaving us to ever forget it, for by my good woman, ye'll have to brighten yerself up if it's only for the sake of yer fine boy."

"Poor Ned," muttered the widow, "poor Ned."

Supping at the beef-tea she droned, "Sure I'm only a drag on him, I only keep him down and God knows he's a good son and deserves better from me."

"Don't talk like that, Mrs. Brady!" remonstrated Mrs. Hanna, "Yer boy needs ye and it's a sin for ye to allow yerself to sink the way ye're doing." The sick woman sipped at the beef-tea but never raised her eyes. "Ye'll have to rouse yerself," continued her friend. "Ye'll have to try and stop fretting about yer man. Ye have yer big boy to look after and it would be worse if ye were left with nobody. For by any mother should be proud of having a son like yer Ned."

The sick woman shook her head and in a weak lamenting voice sobbed, "I know that Mrs. Hanna, but what use am I to the poor lad. Ned is young and strong and has the whole world before him and I'm only a hindrance to him. It was different with Peter. He and me belonged to here. Ned is made for a different world. Peter and me always prayed he would never have to slave and be tied to the Row."

Outside in the street the children yelled near the window and Mrs. Hanna rose to chase them, but Mrs. Brady put the jam-pot away and looking up pleaded, "Ach, don't chase the wee childher. I love to hear them. In the nights that I don't be sleeping I always wish I could only hear them playing," then checking herself she suddenly implored her friend not to tell her son she didn't sleep and remarked despondently, "It's the thoughts I do be having that will be taking me."

"Nonsense," said the visitor cheeringly, "Ye'll see a good many of us down before ye go, ye've many years to live with us yet."

Mrs. Brady lowered her head and joined her thin hands, "I don't want to live. I don't want to live if my health's gone, and I don't want to be a drag on my poor boy. The sooner the good God takes me the better for him and for me. The boy must have his chance, that's what Peter used to say, and God knows Peter sacrificed a lot for him and me, so it's little that I wouldn't do to make the world easier for Peter's son if I could."

While the woman talked thus Mrs. Hanna had been listening to some noise in the street. "Listen," she said as if greatly surprised. "There's a cart coming down the street, isn't it an odd time of the day for one to be coming this way?"

A horse passed the window. There was a loud "Whoa" and in a second Johnny Connor opened the door and entered the kitchen.

Trembling from head to feet Mrs. Brady stood up. She knew her boy had gone up the hill to see Johnny and something told her the mountainy man carried bad news.

"Is there anything wrong?" she asked like a frightened child. The hillman smiled broadly as he assuringly repeated, "Nothing much, nothing much, it's only a sprained ankle he got on the rocks, and I just drove down to tell ye and to bring up his clothes as he will hardly be able to come down here for a few days."

"My poor boy," cried the mother, "My poor boy, why didn't ye bring him home? Why didn't ye bring him home?"

Assuring the frightened woman that the damaged ankle had been well attended and that the jolting of the trap down the hill would have been painful, the hillman saw her making preparations to go to her son. In a short time, she was ready for departure and with a bundle of clothes in her hand said good-bye to Mrs. Hanna as she took her seat in Johnny's cart.

Passing up the Row the neighbours were surprised to see the sick woman in the trap, but lips whispered, "God knows the poor soul needs that wee bit of a change."

Johnny watched his charge with the tail of his eye and thought he saw the widow brighten as they left the big road and began the climb up the steep white lane to the mountain.

She had nothing to say, however, so the hillman did all of the talking. Pointing to this field and that he tried his best to interest her only to discover that below her shawl she had her Rosary beads in her hands, and her lips were moving.

The journey up the steep hill seemed long to Johnny but to Mrs. Brady it appeared unending. At last, they arrived in the yard in front of the cottage and the mountainy man leaped from his cart. Helping the sick woman to reach the ground he led her gently into the kitchen. Mrs.

Brady neither looked to left or right. The hens dashed past her unseen. Only one thought held her and that was of her injured son. To her there was an indefinable joy at hurrying to the boy's side and knowing that he needed her.

Immediately she entered the kitchen her frail shoulders were enfolded by two strong arms and a hearty boyish laugh behind her made her turn her head to look into the beaming eyes of her tall son. The startled mother's eyes rested on the lad's face, then freeing herself from his arms she looked examiningly at his feet. Her boy was well, gladness and pain fought in her heart. She was glad he was sound but pained because she could be of no service. Then she was puzzled and her head began to swim, and body shake.

Ned carefully placed her in a straw bottomed chair and removing her shawl began to explain, "Don't' worry, ma, I'm alright, I've no sprained ankle," he began, "Johnny and me knew ye needed a change. We knew ye liked the top of the hill so we made it appear I was hurt in order to get ye to come. We planned it for ye, ma, Johnny and me planned it for ye," Ned laughed. Johnny approached nearer to the puzzled mother, "We had to do it Mrs. Brady, we had to do it," said the big man soothingly.

"We knew there was no coaxing of ye to take a change and give yerself a chance of getting better so we took this way. It was too bad," he added, "but it just had to be done."

The poor woman tried to smile. Her eyes glanced around the kitchen and then to her thin white fingers and the black beads, "I will be with ye, ma," said Ned enthusiastically, "I have got my holidays and you and me will spend the two weeks with Johnny, we'll be together, we'll be together up here."

Mrs. Brady still fingered her black beads, as her son continued. "The air up here will do ye good. Ye'll be able to get plenty of spring water, fresh eggs and milk, and butter and ma, you and me'll be able to walk about the fields together."

A look of confusion came over the pale face. Raising her eyes a little she protested, "But it's far from the chapel son, it's far from the chapel."

Johnny, however, came to the rescue by saying that he would bring the priest up to see her while she was with him, and this seemed to relieve her.

The young man threw himself wholeheartedly into trying to make his mother's holiday beneficial to her. For years he had dreamed of this opportunity as if in part payment towards all she had done for him. This was only to be a first instalment towards his vast debt to her. Each day he took her out amongst the hens and ducks and let her stroke the cows. *How many years had passed since she had stroked a cow?*

To the wee hidden spring well from which she and his father had drank in their courting days he brought her, and when he had filled his hands with the crystal water for her to drink, he knew she was thinking.

On the heather the son and mother rested and in the fields the lad gathered bunches of wild flowers for her to carry back to her room. Full of enthusiasm the excited boy danced attendance on his mother and after a few days was rewarded by seeing a little colour come to her face and a bright gleam appear in her eyes.

"No wonder Peter used to love this hill," she muttered repeatedly, as she looked down on the smoky town and thought of her departed husband.

"Peter loved here, Peter loved here" she said somewhat sadly at almost every spot where she paused to rest, until her son began to imagine he could hear those words ringing all over the big hill. Poor boy, he little knew, as he led her through the grass and along the wee paths, that the flushes coming to her pale pained face had another meaning, nor did he know the sick woman never slept at night. For a long time the poor mother had been unable to close an eye. The loss of her bright burly husband had left her bed lonely and full of thoughts. Each night, for years, she had nestled into Peter's big broad back and prayed silently on her beads as he fell sound asleep from the exertions of the day. Then when she had said all her prayers for him and her son, the beads were tucked carefully beneath the pillow and nestling her face against her man's warm shoulders she was lulled asleep by the rhythm of his heavy breathing.

All this had passed with the death of Peter and her sleep had gone with him. Since then, she prayed on her beads throughout each night. When she had been eight days at Johnny's Connor's home on the dark hill Mrs. Brady suddenly grew weaker and could not leave her bed. The doctor was summoned, and Father Mick came up to prepare her for her last journey.

"Please don't tell my boy Ned, I'm not going to get better," the poor soul pleaded to both doctor and priest. Johnny's home became as silent as the grave. The fowl were no longer allowed to enter the kitchen and the feeding place was changed to the far end of the yard. The doctor had taken Ned aside and told him his mother's days were numbered and the poor lad was broken-hearted. Through his tears he implored the doctor, priest and his friend Johnny not to tell his mother she was not going to recover. Muttering prayers to herself and occasionally saying to the black roof of her room, "Peter loved here next to heaven, Peter loved here." The sick fading woman lay in bed with her dark rosary clutched in her frail white hands.

The wallet of notes her fine son had saved and treasured for her holiday had now lost its value. His mother was leaving him before he could let her know how much he loved her and the notes he had so carefully saved to give her life would now be used to bury her.

"A saint, Ned, a saint Ned, yer mother was always a saint," said Johnny Connor consolingly, as he and his young friend walked from the door with Father Mick after the priest's last visit to the dying woman.

"True for you Johnny," remarked his reverence, "True for you and there are many more like her being hurried to early graves by the way of living that's down there," pointing to the town, "God alone knows it's a terrible martyrdom for good men or good women. We're all in it Johnny," he added sadly, "And there seems to be nothing for us to do but try and make the best of it by endeavouring to love and help one another here and join one another hereafter."

The mountainy man shook his head, "Feth Father," he began clearing his throat, "It's only one in thousands can do that and there's some people it would be hard to love while the millions who can't make the best of it get the crumbs and the torture and find them hard."

The hillman was trying to control a growing temper. Then after a pause he asked, "Is it not because of a hope of relief sometime in life rather than the promise of reward in death that the poor working people tolerate their lot with such patience Father?" The priest smiled, "And what way would you have it Johnny?"

"Have it, what way would I have it. By my soul I would have it right," began the angry hillman, "I would see that they got what they were entitled to in this life and that those who grinded them for profits got what they deserved here too."

Some say hard work had ennobled people" remarked the priest dryly.

Johnny raised his eyebrows and gave a sigh, "That's alright, Father, but I notice it's only those who haven't to do any hard work that mostly talk that way. Twelve hours a day in stuffy mills with a pay that would barely keep a dog isn't work at all, it's slaughter."

The young priest brightened. He liked to hear Johnny talking. Johnny's voice was so rich in feeling, he thought. "But, the most of the people seem to get through somehow," he remarked encouragingly.

The mountainy man's face reddened. Across his eyes seemed to travel a film of the painful scenes he had witnessed through the years. His lips drew tight together, "Listen to the coughs ye be hearing in the church on a Sunday morning and ye'll realise what it costs them," he said angrily, "Look at the pale faces of the childher, look at the size of their homes and the dirt of the streets look at the ages on the tombstones in the cemetery and then tell me would ye like to have to live like them?" he asked.

Without waiting for an answer, the big man continued. "You yerself were talking about Saints one Sunday, why it's enough to turn saints into devils."

"But the people are good," said Father Mick with emphasis on the "are".

Johnny's eyes blazed as he looked down at the town and then at the priest, "Good, why there never was better, but there's nobody seems to want goodness rewarded in this life the reward for goodness is after ye die. The poor people are perfect, they're the milk of human kindness," stretching his clenched hand, "But, take it from me what they are being forced to endure will make them worse than devils and they'll eventually turn on those who say they must remain hungry and must remain slaves or who call starvation blessed in a world of plenty."

Father Mick laughed. "You're hard on everybody Johnny," he remarked jokingly but the mountainy man still frowned and resumed talking, "Honestly, I can't help losing my temper when I see what's going on around me and I believe that the great God is not going to ask his people if they hugged a girl too tight or stole a sixpence, but will expect some account of how we all resisted the destruction of his race made to his image and likeness. When I see the best of mankind deprived of its freedom and ground to ill-health and short life in hellish conditions, I'm convinced there will be a time of reckoning for it sometime, and enraged working people will arise from it all."

The priest became grave, "I realise Johnny the whole way of living is entirely wrong but what can you or I do to change it? As it is we seem to be caught in it ourselves and although we may rebel what can we do? It would seem to me we can only go on wheeling our barrows and praying."

Having accompanied his reverence almost half-way towards the town Johnny and Ned stopped to turn back. The young man had not spoken on the journey nor did the two older men expect him. After shaking hands with his friends, the priest continued the journey down the steep hill and as he reviewed the remarks of the mountainy man he thought of the miracles of the wine, loaves and fishes, the falling Manna, and the injunction of *feed my lambs, feed my sheep,* while Johnny and Ned travelled back up the hill to the dying mother.

CHAPTER TWENTY-FIVE

The Exile's Return

Sheila McCann's Aunt Margaret died in the month of May leaving a lot of money to her young niece, and the girl arrived back in Belfast on the 14th of July. In Ravage's Row there was rejoicing and people came from far and near to visit the McCann house and greet the returned emigrant.

'Isn't she lovely?', 'She's just herself', 'She's not a bit changed', 'She hasn't forgotten herself', were the verdicts of the people and it was a relief to all that the girl did not talk 'Yanky'. To them this was the proof she had not forgotten the old homestead or the people.

The great fortune of the McCann's became the topic of general conversation and many of the neighbours expressed the opinion that the family would soon be removing to one of the big houses on the front of the road. "Thank God to see ye back again," was the greeting the girl Sheila received from Johnny Connor when she came out to the milkman's cart on the morning following her return to Ravage's Row.

"Thanks Johnny leave us a pint," she said, blushingly extending a pink jug to the big man who stared at her. "Yer horse is very quiet now Johnny," remarked the girl, in an effort to free herself from the hillman's examining eyes.

"He's trying to be content with his miserable lot," answered Johnny still watching her and measuring the milk at the same time.

The big man's eyes wanted to linger on her. She was radiant, she was like a hill in sunshine, then he thought of the clouds on Ned Brady's young face.

The returned girl was happy, happy, he thought, to be back home but happier at being able to bring help to her mother and her little brothers and sisters with the money left her. The experience of seeing her family get more food and clothes had brought a new joy to the young girl's heart, and her dark curls danced gleefully about her dancing eyes.

"Everybody'll be glad to see ye back in the oul' home," remarked Johnny, filling the jug, and preparing to drive off. Suddenly the dark curls became motionless and the bright eyes steady as the young girl enquired, "How is poor Mrs. Brady, Johnny? I heard she was up on the hill with you and that she had to have the priest."

This was the opportunity the mountainy man had been hoping for. He saw that the girl's face had become clouded like a hill before a shower, so he explained there was little hope of Mrs. Brady ever getting well again.

Johnny knew that Ned Brady and she had not been corresponding while she was in America, but being fond of both the young people, had decided to try and bring them together again. Having some acquaintance with horses he knew that thoroughbreds sometimes shied for very little reason. In Sheila's beautiful eyes he saw tears as she stammered: "I'm very sorry, please tell Mrs. Brady I was asking for her."

He was in the act of referring to Ned Brady when a polite voice called, "Hello Sheila you're welcome back," and Luggy Moran began a conversation with the girl. Johnny cursed into himself and wishing the girl, "Good Morning," drove down the street shouting back "I'll see ye another time, Sheila." He was disappointed at having been deprived of the opportunity he had been hoping for and almost said loudly, "Damn that upsetting brat," to the next customer.

On his rounds everyone enquired about Mrs. Brady, and some sent little presents which he gladly carried back in his cart. As he drove from door to door, he could not forget Ned and his dying mother up on the hill, and when serving Liza, the publican, he decided that Barney Bubbles and Billy Clarke were both lucky to be able to forget their lot now and then in booze. Leaving Liza's door, he reasoned when things are sore with them some rushed to God and some to drink. The pubs were there ready and waiting. Many of the publicans in fact tried to make saints of their poorly paid and hard wrought young country assistants and some forced them to go to confession regularly because they found it cheaper to get God to watch them than to pay an accountant.

"Poor Ned Brady," he groaned as he drove along, "Wouldn't it be a blessing if ye could get drunk until yer poor mother had passed into the next world."

That night, Johnny and Ned sat by the bedside of the dying widow, Johnny's eldest daughter Rose, who was so reserved, she rarely approached when her father had visitors, had taken up the duties of nurse. "She's just a home-bird," was how Johnny described her if anyone remarked the girl. Before he and his mother had come to the hill, Ned Brady had only seen Johnny's daughter once or twice, but at no time had he heard the sound of her voice. She was like a nun, he had thought. With her, home was her habit. Johnny, Rose and Ned watched the bed. With straining eyes, the young man scanned the face of his mother and felt a silent gratitude for the care of Johnny's daughter... As he sat in the broad earthen-floored room with its straw-bottomed chairs, its high wooden bed and darkened straw covered roof, he communed with himself. A few more days, maybe a few more hours, then I shall lose her forever, and be alone in the world.

His ambition had been to ease her burden and bring her joy. Now that he could give her a little more it was too late just like his dream for his father. The new grey shawl had never been worn. The trip he had promised to give her to her childhood haunts would never materialise. The future he had planned had collapsed. Amongst the ruins he saw only the wee while altar. Yes, he had got her that and she had used it. He was proud and thankful as he recalled the expression on her pale face when it arrived and pictured her kneeling form beside it. Often. she had knelt there but for whom had she prayed? Forgetting herself she had prayed for her dead husband and for her living son. It was the altar of her sacrifice. As he sat, thinking in the silence, the sound of a weak voice came from the bed, "Don't be staying there, son," it said, "I'll be alright, go and take yer rest, go and take yer rest, ye need yer rest."

Ned had never heard his mother's voice sound so weakly. It seemed to come from a distance as if she had already left him, and he shook as he answered, assuringly, "I'm alright ma, I would rather be here." But the sick mother was not satisfied. Looking towards where Johnny Connor sat, she pleaded to the hillman, "Please Johnny, make him go and rest, I'll be alright but he's young and needs his sleep."

Johnny got up from his chair and saying convincingly, "Alright Mrs. Brady don't worry, I'll make him lie down," took the son by the arm and led him out of the room. In the kitchen he pointed to a chair by the window whispering, "You sit on that like a good chap and don't let her know ye are there."

Tired from his long day's work, the hillman then went to bed after giving instructions to be called if needed, while Rose kept watch by the bedside of Mrs. Brady. Ned sat silently in the kitchen to be rewarded now and then by a whisper from the girl as she came out of the room to report. What a lovely sympathetic voice she had, and how good she is, thought the young man. Since his mother had arrived on the hill Rose Connor had been so attentive, so patient and so kind he was overcome with gratefulness.

How could he ever repay both her and Johnny for all their kindness? He often asked himself.

That was his mother's voice, Yes, it was; what was she saying? He listened, and, from the silence of the room came like a faint prayer, "It's so high up here, it's so high up here, it's so close to the sky." Rose was moistening her lips with a wet spoon. He heard a soft movement of feet. His mother spoke again, "It's so near to heaven, it's so near to heaven," the faint voice repeated. Rose said something but a moan from his mother made it impossible for him to know what it was. Then the sick woman spoke again, "Be kind to my Ned, be kind to my Ned." Tears fell down the lad's cheeks as he sat listening. He fancied he could hear his father voice softly humming, *'Let us sing of the days that are gone Maggie, when you and I were young'.*

The mother spoke, "He's a good boy, no mother ever had a better son." Tears blinded him. He wanted to shout. "No son ever had a better mother," but he bit his lips and let the tears fall.

Johnny Connor had now fallen asleep and from the far room came the sound of his snores to stir the painful thoughts in the young man's head. A queer quietness settled on the sick room, and Ned sat pondering on his short past life. Hunting far back into his childhood he strove to trace every day spent with his parents and every sorrow and joy they had shared together. Then Rose came quietly from the room. Sitting down in a chair on the opposite side of the fireplace she whispered, "She's sleeping; she's sleeping." The lad felt his body relax and both sat silent.

Except for an occasional snore from Johnny's room, no noise disturbed the peacefulness of the mountain home. With her hands joined on her lap and her head bowed the girl appeared to be engaged in prayer. As he peered through the dim light of the room Ned Brady realised for the first time how pretty Rose of the mountain really was.

"My Peter, my Ned," a weak rambling voice called affectionately from the sick room. It came from the heart. The girl rose from her seat and glided from the kitchen.

The lad rose and followed her. In the light of the low lamp, he saw Johnny's daughter place a crucifix in this mother's thin hands. The girl dropped on her knees to pray.

"Pray for us sinners now and at the hour of our death," she repeated. The bed shook with her emotion. Ned leant over her and listening noticed his mother's breathing had grown weaker. Trying to pray he heard the dying woman mutter, "So high up here, so high up here." The snore of the sleeping hillman came from the far room. The dog cried outside in the yard. Ned fell upon his knees and through his tears watched his mother's face. "So near to heaven Peter loved here, so near to heaven," the faintest voice murmured.

There was a slight movement on the pillow and the lad's slave mother had left him forever and had gone to join her Peter.

CHAPTER TWENTY-SIX

"Next Stop Heaven"

"It's surprising – the number of the upper class that visit the McCann's now-a-days," remarked Barney Bubbles the rougher as occasionally a round bubble darted from his tongue and flew away.

With several men, he was standing outside the church on the Sunday following the death of the widow Brady. "Since wee Sheila came back from America with the money I've noticed that myself," said his friend Billy Clarke, somewhat seriously.

Barney Bubbles smiled. Then he gave a funny cough, chuckled and shot a string of bubbles in the air. "They're tripping over one another to get into McCann's wee home now, they're not afraid of dirtying their clothes."

The young priest, Father Mick passing out of the church on his way down the steps called "Good morning, men." "I don't see that young clergyman down in the Row so often," remarked Billy, looking after his reverence.

"No," explained his friend, "he's not influenced by the money, his hearts in the right place."

"Hunting for money changes the best of them," a rougher remarked, but Barney Bubbles shook his head as he said pleasantly, "It's not the hunting, it's the getting of it."

"It's a great thing this money altogether," grunted Billy Clarke.

"Aye, aye," chuckled Barney Bubbles, "We're all like bees, we like to flock near the honey."

Billy Clarke rattled the two pennies which his wife had given him for chapel-money and which he had thought better to keep and said thoughtfully, "Some people discover where the honey is early and some of us never find out."

Fissy Burns, was bursting to say something. He was a big hearty fellow who would have liked to save but liked the whisky better, so the whisky always won. Extending his thick red lips blabbered, "I heard a fellow say some people's noses could smell money because their noses were cut to scent it."

Barney Bubbles had no respect for Fissy's intelligence or opinions and looking quickly at his friend Billy Clarke he continued, "Putting all alleged jokes aside Billy, isn't it funny how our wee homes and clothes are never inviting to the aristocracy until there's money in them and then they're attractive."

"Good for ye Barney," said one of the men encouragingly. The rougher took a deep breath and resumed, "Any other time, our streets and ourselves are dirty. But when the cash gets into them, they become spotless. Why the oul doctor even stops in the Row to talk to the McCann children now and I remember a short time ago he was afraid they'd touch his clothes."

"Oul' Aunt Margaret's money made them nicer people to the people who never thought they were nice before," drawled Billy Clarke sarcastically.

Everybody laughed. In a restless humour Barney Bubbles shuffled his feel and spoke seriously, "Man dear, if there was money instead of poverty in every home in the Row ye couldn't keep the gentry out of it with a red-hot poker, they'd be falling over one another trying to lick us."

"It's changed days," groaned Billy Clarke, "None of them ever cared to come down the street until the McCann's got the money, and they never liked meeting any of our kind. They don't mind taking yer money, but if they met ye down the town they wouldn't bid ye the time of day."

"Aye and them living on us," qualified Fissy Burns loudly. "Wheest, wheest," commanded Barney Bubbles, "Here comes Father Mick and Sheila McCann."

The young priest and the returned girl approached the group of men. "Well, my men what's the discussion this morning?" asked his reverence.

"Work, work," answered two voices without hesitation. Instinctively the men knew that doctors, and mill-owners and some clergymen expected the poor to concern themselves only about work.

"Is any of you men going up the hill this morning?" asked his reverence looking from one to the other. "Yes Father," replied Billy Clarke, Barney is going up to bring down some well water for oul' Liza's rheumatism."

"That's just grand," commented the priest addressing the rougher. "Sheila here is going up to Johnny Connor's to bring me some fresh eggs and butter, which I forgot about yesterday and you will be company for her Barney."

The rougher coughed with surprise but was soon talking to the young girl. The priest began to chat with the other men and as the conversation became animated Barney Bubbles slipped off with Sheila on their journey to the hilltop.

 The girl was delighted with her company but for some time the rougher was embarrassed. Often, he used to say, "I'm no good with the women," but strangely enough the women liked him, and Sheila chatted lightly as they walked along together. Gradually he got used to his 'swell company' and his tongue loosened.

Question followed question. 'Isn't it a nice morning?', 'Are ye glad to be home again?', 'How did ye like America?', and 'Did ye ever run across so-an'-so?' and others were showered on the girl as soon as he had got his second wind and got used to his company.

As they turned off the broad road and came in full view of the big hill the eyes of the girl searched greedily for the wee white cottage high up near the summit. In America, she had often pictured the dark green hill, the narrow while lane running from its foot and Johnny Connor's mountain home resting near the sky. Often. she had wept for a sight of it. Often too she had thought of the man beside her and his funny little bubbles.

"Johnny's house looks very high up from here," she remarked admiringly, when she had at last located the small, thatched home that looked like a tiny baby-toy on the massive hill in the distance.

"I hope I'm able to make it," said the rougher coughing "We were on Irish flax last week and it's severe on the chest."

The girl looking pityingly at her companion and was preparing to speak when he gave a laugh and briskly continued, "It does a fellow good to have a walk up the hill on a Sunday. It clears the lungs of the pouse or as poor Peter Brady used to say, 'it chases away the cobwebs'."

As the rougher walked and talked by her side, Sheila's eyes rested on the far away cottage and the name Brady caused a lump to gather in her pretty throat. Her thoughts brought a dimness to her sight. Since returning she had learned how young Ned Brady had watched over his dying mother on the hill, and that morning was told the broken-hearted young man had gone away to Dublin after the burial of his last parent. Then as she found herself wondering if Sylvia Bennington would also be in Dublin her companion remarked, "It's a long time since ye were up this way."

They had entered the steep straight white lane and the brightness of the limestone in the sun dazzled the girl. "It is, it is," she replied excitedly suddenly recalling her last and only walk with young Ned Brady.

"It's a bit rough – not like the smooth up-to-date roads ye saw in America," continued her companion.

Barney Bubbles did not understand the joy of seeing that rough white road again. After having been three thousand miles away and thinking it would never meet the eyes again. He had never been out of Ireland, the girl reasoned, as she smiled sadly. How beautiful it all seemed to her after having been so far away. How often she had recalled that steep white way with its green hedges, and, with it, the tall lithe figure and handsome bright face of Ned Brady. When she had learned he was keeping company with Sylvia Bennington and when she did not get any reply to a long letter, she had sent him, she had tried to think of the big green hill without him but found it impossible.

The big dark hill and Ned Brady had become inseparately connected in her mind. The song of a bird on a bush close by aroused her from her thoughts. Jumping excitedly towards her companion she plucked the rougher's sleeve and asked, "What kind of a bird is that Barney?"

The songster was startled. Rising from its bough it flew across the road as the man explained it was a robin. Could it be the same wee robin that had sung for Ned and her when they had walked that way? She wondered, but did not ask her friend lest he should laugh. A moistness gathered in her eyes and the steepness of the road was unnoticed. Once, her friend paused at the most difficult part of the brae but mopping his brow and taking a deep breath he grunted, "It must be done," and resumed the climb.

Arriving, near the yard of Johnny Connor's mountain home Barney Bubbles complained about his heart palpitating like an engine remarking humorously, "It's bad enough when the lungs go but when the oul' ticker goes it's all up." However, he led the way with a confident swing until they reached Johnny's door where he flung himself down upon a box beneath the window and jokingly swore he would not leave it for a week.

Johnny Connor, who had been near at hand, greeted his visitors with enthusiasm and brought them into the house in spite of the rougher's protests to be allowed to remain and die in peace where he was. The tired townsman had barely sufficient time to have himself comfortably seated inside, however, when his mountainy friend approached his chair and grabbing him by the shoulder practically dragged him to the door saying, "Come on Barney, I want to show ye a new cow I've got in the byre."

Just then the rougher would have liked to say. "To blazes with ye and yer new cow," but a wink from the hillman's eye made him resign himself with curiosity.

"Ye can have a seat there Sheila and go and get some heather when ye're rested," Johnny called to the girl as the two men left the house and moved towards the byre.

"Heather," what thoughts the mention of it brought to the girl as she sat alone in the big country kitchen and listened to the tramp, tramp of the departing feet across the yard. When the sound had died away and silence came, the spirit of poor Mrs. Brady seemed to come out from the room in which she died. Knowing the poor woman must have died in there the young girl tried to visualise the last moments of the dying mother and burned with sympathy for her lonely son.

For some time, she sat pondering and waiting. Outside the wild birds sang on the bushes and the fowl flocked about the door. Now and then she strained to catch the sound of the voices or steps of the men, but in vain. Thoughts of the dead woman haunted her. Almost an hour went by and as if urged by the spirit of Mrs. Brady that seemed to come from the room each time her eyes rested on the door, she rose from her chair and leaving the house set out in quest of a bunch of heather. Over the same wee path, hammered visible by the mountain sheep, she had tripped behind Ned Brady.

The heather tickled her pretty legs. An inviting clump beckoned. Bending down she began to pull when something moved behind a large whin bush in front of her. Her heart stopped beating. Then straightening herself she looked in the direction of the noise. A lark sang wildly above her. A little rabbit jumped rashly past. The songster above tempted her to look, but she resisted. The flash of the rabbit dragged at her eyes, but they were riveted. On the other side of the whin bush a young man had stood up. She only saw his shoulders and his pale face, but she swayed with weakness. The heather fell from hands as he stepped towards her. It was Ned Brady.

In a few minutes the re-united young couple had sat down together, and the lad learned for the first time how Sheila had waited and waited on a reply to a letter she had sent to Bennington's for him, and which must have arrived after he had left and been kept by the angry Sylvia, thus accounting for her scented note about 'something of great interest'.

A cough sounded from below, then the laughter of passing men. The young people looked. Far down on the hill's slope Johnny Connor stood smiling and waving a stick. Beside him stood Barney Bubbles the rougher calling loudly through his hands:

"Next Stop Heaven, Next Stop Heaven!"

- The End -

❅ ❅ ❅

PHOTOS

Cahal (Center) In Irish Republican Training Camp - Antrim 1919

The Three Bradley Brothers; Cahal(Front Right), Hugh(Top Left), Peter (Front Left)

Cahal's Father Charles Bradley's Name On The First Republican Burial Plot In Milltown Cemetary, West Belfast

The Bradley Grave Which Holds 18 Family Members, West Belfast

Cahal Bradley's Resting Place, Milltown Cemetary, West Belfast

Holy Cross Chapel, Crumlin Road, North Belfast

'Motionless Dark Green Coloured Whale' - As It Is Referred To In The Book . Black Mountains Pictured In The Distance.

ACKNOWLEDGEMENT

I would like to thank the following people dearly for helping me throughout the process of publishing the book 'Next Stop Heaven'.

Jim Gibney

Micky Ligget

Joe Lavery, Genealogist

Fr. Gary Donegan, Holy Cross Church

Colum Gallagher

The Feile 2015

Printers: Nova Print

Ardoyne Kickhams GAA

Belfast Taxi C.I.C King Street

Pat's Printers

My family: Lynn Bradley and children Caitlin, Jaide, Amber Rose, and Charlie Bradley

The extended Bradley family

Printed in Great Britain
by Amazon

29727614R00149